Saint Augustine

S. Augustine the preacher

Being fifty short sermon notes founded upon select passages from his writings

Saint Augustine

S. Augustine the preacher
Being fifty short sermon notes founded upon select passages from his writings

ISBN/EAN: 9783337264789

Printed in Europe, USA, Canada, Australia, Japan

Cover: Foto ©Raphael Reischuk / pixelio.de

More available books at **www.hansebooks.com**

Patristic Sermons.

Vol. I.

S. Augustine.

S. AUGUSTINE THE PREACHER;

BEING

FIFTY SHORT SERMON NOTES

FOUNDED UPON

SELECT PASSAGES FROM HIS WRITINGS.

BY

JOHN M. ASHLEY, B.C.L.
VICAR OF FEWSTON,

LONDON:

J. T. HAYES, 17, HENRIETTA STREET, COVENT GARDEN;
AND LYALL PLACE, EATON SQUARE.
MDCCCLXXVII.

LONDON:
SWIFT AND CO., NEWTON STREET, HIGH HOLBORN, W.C.

BIOGRAPHICAL NOTICE.

S. AUGUSTINE was born at Tagaste, a town of Numidia, November 13th, A.D. 354. Monica, his mother, early enrolled him among the Order of the Catechumens. Patricius, his father, educated him first at Tagaste, and afterwards at Madaura. In 371 he went to Carthage, where he studied Rhetoric with much success. The *Hortensius* of Cicero imbued him with his first love of philosophy, and led to his earnest study of Holy Scripture, after which he fell away to Manichæism for a time. In 373 Augustine returned to Tagaste, and taught Rhetoric and practised at the bar; and in 379 he went to Carthage, and afterwards became Professor of Rhetoric at Rome, at which place, having been badly used by his pupils, on the recommendation of Symmachus, the Prefect of the city, he was appointed Professor at Milan. It was at Milan that S. Augustine listened to the sublime teaching and preaching of S. Ambrose, the Bishop of that city, and was converted by him from Manichæism to pure

Christianity. As soon as possible Augustine renounced his Professorship, betook himself to the reverent study of Holy Scripture and the Platonic dialogues, and was baptized by S. Ambrose on Easter Day, 387. After his baptism S. Augustine left Milan, went back to Rome, saw the last of his mother at Ostia, and arrived at Tagaste 388; in which place he remained for three years, leading a strictly religious life. Valerius, Bishop of Hippo, ordained him Priest 391; and he was consecrated Coadjutor-Bishop of Hippo, by Megalius, the Primate of Numidia, in 395. He died August 28, 430, at the age of seventy-six years, a striking example that the system of Church Patronage was not more perfect in the fifth century than it is in the nineteenth. The fact remains, with its lesson for all time, that Augustine, the most eloquent, learned, holy ecclesiastic of his own or of any other day, as well as the most voluminous writer, was left to languish for thirty-five years of his precious life in an obscure Numidian diocese. The materials for the life of S. Augustine are largely contained in his own writings; especially in his City of God, Confessions, Retractations, and Epistles. The moral of the life of S. Augustine lies in the fact that his earliest and purest faith lay dormant for years in his soul, obscured by heathen studies and false doctrine, and at length germinated into a second and more glorious growth, producing those fruits unto holiness of which we are become the partakers, through the instrumentality of his writings.

PREFACE.

THE following pages are the expression of a plan which has been long matured. It was first, in a shorter form than the present one, applied to the Apostolic Fathers and S. Clement of Alexandria, in a series of papers which appeared in a Religious Review some twenty years ago; having been suggested in the first instance by the perusal of Vivien's "Tertullianus Prædicans," and Coleridge's "Aids to Reflection." To utilize and to popularize in any way the vast treasures of learning which are stored up in the writings of the Fathers, will never be deemed an unworthy work, by those who from their scholarship and knowledge of them are the best judges both of their merits and defects. The writings of the Fathers are the great literary heritage of the Church; which, strange as it may seem to say so, is, nevertheless, a personal possession of but few of her children. This

may be, because most of the editions of the Fathers
are both costly and cumbrous ; or it may be, because
after entering upon the active duties of life, continued
and laborious study is well-nigh out of the question.
From whatsoever cause, the fact remains the same,
that few of our parochial clergy have either the leisure
or the aptitude for patristic studies. Hence the
opening which is afforded for a little book like the
present, to fill up some small gap in the theological
literature of the day. To any who desire to obtain an
introduction to the writings of S. Augustine, the
"Exposition of the Sermon on the Mount, drawn from
the writings of St. Augustine, with an introductory Essay on his merits as an interpreter of Holy
Scripture," by Archbishop Trench, cannot be too
strongly recommended. If carefully read, it will be
found to unfold a large portion of the mind of
Augustine, and to leave with the reader a profound
sense of his spirituality, depth of thought, and truly
Christian humility of thought. The book of Archbishop Trench is referred to because it stands in aim
and object, and, alas ! in many other particulars also,
in contrast with the present little book, which is not
devoted to the unfolding of any particular line of

Augustinian thought, but to a humbler purpose, the utilization of a few of those particular ideas and reflections which so abound in the pages of this truly great theologian. To procure the passages which are treated of hereafter, all the works of S. Augustine have been read, a process which occupied from four to six months. During the perusal, any passage or expression which attracted particular attention was noted down, and most generally commented upon at the time. The considerations which determined the selection of the quotations to be used, were : Firstly, the clear and striking statement of some great truth in a few words. Secondly, the relation which such passages bear to subjective and ethical rather than to dogmatic truth. Had it been wished to found a series of dogmatic sermons upon S. Augustine, nothing would have been easier than to turn to the "Index Rerum," where, under their several headings, all that was required might be found at a glance. Recourse was had to the Index for one sermon only (The Types of the Church, Ser. vii. p. 26) ; and such use does not seem to have formed the happiest sermon of the series. Thirdly, when a fragmentary thought or expression full of meaning, seemed capable of expansion without loss of power. Fourthly, when anything was found more than ordinarily suggestive in any of those minor Treatises of Augustine which are so much less read than his well-known works "De Consensu;" "De Trinitate;" "Confessiones," or the "De Civitate Dei," etc. It was desirable also to obtain as much variety as possible in the chosen subjects, thus selecting some which are more spiritual, and others which are more moral and thoughtful. Books of this description are necessarily tentative, and therefore must be contained within certain limits, or nothing would have been easier than to have multiplied the Augustinian extracts by three or four, and to have expanded the notes in a corresponding ratio. The difficulty of composition arose in this case not from lack of matter, but from the need there was of strict condensation ; which although carried as far as possible, it will be hoped has not led to obscurity. Hence, the few remarks which are appended to the quotations from S. Augustine, contain little more than the germs of thought, which may be variously used in the preparation for the pulpit—a preparation which has been pronounced by one justly venerated amongst men of every grade and of every opinion, as a states-man, a scholar, and an orator, to be " the accumulation and thorough digestion of knowledge." With a view to the former part of pulpit preparation, as thus defined by Mr. Gladstone—"the accumulation of knowledge "—these simple sketches of sermon thoughts are put forth. It is earnestly trusted that they may in some degree fulfil the purpose which is implied in their publication; for should they be found to do so, it is intended to treat others of the Fathers in a like manner. The present little book then, is put forth as an experiment, and it was deemed advisable to commence the series of " Patristic Sermons " with Augustine, because he is one of the most difficult of the Fathers to turn to profitable account in sermon-making. Turning to his works during the composition of a sermon, it is seldom that a reference furnishes anything available; it is so different with Tertullian, or Origen, or S. Gregory the Great; their pages are seldom or ever consulted in vain. This peculiarity in Augustine may be accounted for, partly from the fact that he is very diffuse in his style, allowing his current of thought to run away hither and thither, wheresoever a text of Scripture quoted in illustration of his subject may lead him; and partly from the rapidity and energy of his thoughts, which hardly allow themselves

words wherewith they can be expressed. "Melioris
avidus sum quo sæpe fruor interius, antequam eum
explicare verbis sonantibus cæpero, quod ubi minus
quam mihi motus est evaluero, contristor linguam
meam cordi meo non prorse sufficere. Totum enim
quod intelligo, volo ut qui me audit intelligat,
et sentio mea non ita loqui, ut hoc efficiam."
(*De Catec. Rud.* vol. iv. p. 261, G.) It is most true
that the speech of S. Augustine at times seems all
insufficient to express the rapid and burning thoughts
that ever and anon flit across his brain. There is no
writer, perhaps, who demands more thought in the
reader than he does, in order to fill up and supply his
lacunæ of expression. In fact, nearly all his treatises
are suggestive rather than exhaustive; and they open
out various trains of thought which are often very far
removed from the matter in hand. Therefore was the
experiment made first upon S. Augustine, for it was
felt that if he could be utilized for preaching purposes,
it would be a much easier task to apply the same
treatment to some other of the Fathers. Another
purpose which this little book has in view, is to induce,
if possible, some of its readers to study the works of
S. Augustine for themselves; for which study they

will be most fully and amply repaid. In his pages they will find beauties of thought and expression, and above all of Scriptural exegesis at which any thoughtful mind cannot but delight and marvel—beauties carrying with them truths of the highest import and significance. Moreover, in the systematic study of a great theological writer, and one also writing in a foreign language, there is a certain mental effort implied which is very healthful and disciplinal to the mind, and one which tends in no small degree to the retention of that which has been so acquired.

With regard to the works of S. Augustine themselves, a few hints and notices may not be altogether unacceptable or out of place as introductory to the following pages. "The Confessions," are universally known and admired, and if they are read in conjunction with those of Rousseau, also with Goethe's Autobiography, and Newman's "Apologia," a vast and varied insight will be obtained into the workings of the human heart under four widely-contrasted spheres of life. "The City of God," which occupied thirteen years in its composition, is perhaps the most learned and finished of all S. Augustine's works ; but with the exception of the three last books, is not of much value

to the theological student, at least, at the beginning
of his studies. For devotional reading, the Explanation or "Enarration of the Psalms" stands alone;
especially those portions of it which were delivered
orally as expositional homilies. It is next to impossible
to overrate the value and richness of this treatise,
which seems to reach a far higher standard of exegesis
than even the Tractates or Homilies upon S. John.
The several "Questions" are very pleasant reading;
both the eighty-three Questions and the eight addressed
to Dulcitius, as are also those upon some of the
earlier historical books of the Old Testament. They
can be read at any time, and the answers pondered
over one by one. The four books on Christian
Doctrine are, on the whole, recommended to those
persons who take up S. Augustine for the first time;
especially the last book, which treats of the teaching
exposition of Holy Scripture. The "Enchiridion,"
written for Laurence, a Roman lord, might well be
read either with or immediately after the "De Doc-
trinâ." There is not one of its eighty-seven chapters
which does not contain something worthy of remem-
brance. "The Christian Combat" ("De Agone
Christiano") is also an interesting little treatise, com-

prised in thirty-three sections, showing very plainly
how sin can be wrestled with and overcome. The
purely controversial writings of S. Augustine against
the Manichees, the Donatists, the Pelagians, and
others, as well as his polemical treatise on the Trinity,
may, without irreverence to so great a man, be said
to be almost obsolete at the present day. Not so his
Epistles, numbering two hundred and thirty letters,
which, though often touching upon merely local or
personal matters, have a freshness and reality about
them that must always interest the reader. Frequent
use has been made of them in the present book. If
neither so spiritual nor so matured as his later productions there is a charm about the earlier works of S.
Augustine which is all their own. No one can read
the treatise "Contra Academicos" without gaining
many a useful thought, most purely and elegantly
expressed, and the dogma of Cicero, that we really
know nothing, is well and ably refuted. These
three books "Against the Academics," containing in
all forty-three chapters, were written in solitude, away
from Milan, during the time that S. Augustine was
preparing himself to receive the Sacrament of Baptism.
The book "Of a Happy Life" ("De vitâ beatâ,")

composed in the thirty-third year of his age, and dedi-
cated to his Milan friend, Manilius Theodorus, is very
dramatic and racy in style. It contains a spirited
introduction which describes three classes of navigators
sailing upon the sea of life, and which is followed by
three dialogues, the conclusion of the whole being that
true happiness consists in the knowledge of God. That
since none but God can fill the soul, none but God can
make it happy. In the two books on "Providence"
("De Ordine") there are four dialogues, all fairly
dramatic. The third contains an instructive explanation as to what it is to be with God ; how the good
abide with Him, and so become in a certain sense unchangeable. The two books of the "Soliloquies"
("Soliloquiorum libri"), which leave the work un-
finished, were also written by S. Augustine before his
baptism. The second book furnishing a good illustration of his habit of digression. In it, he is speaking of
the immortality of the soul, which he affirms to be
eternal, because it is the habitation of truth. He then
indulges upon a series of reflections upon truth and
falsehood, which occupy the remainder of the book.
Of course, it is not for a moment intended to assert
that any of these earlier works are of the same moment

or value as the one hundred and thirty-four homilies
which form the Commentaries upon the Gospel or First
Epistle of S. John; the "Enarration of the Psalms;"
and the "De Consensu Evangelistarum," with its two
hundred and eighty-four sections; nor can we put them
down as equal to the lesser Tractates of his later years,
such as those upon "Christian Discipline," "The
New Song," "The Conflict of the Soul," and others;
yet, if not so solid, they have a greater eloquence and
a livelier play of the imagination than mark any of the
more mature productions of his pen. With regard to
the text of S. Augustine, the first accurate recension
of it was made by the Doctors of Louvain, whose
valuable edition of his works was printed at Antwerp
in 1577. No less than six editions of this recension
were printed at Paris within eighty years of the
appearance of the Antwerp edition, which was also
reprinted at Venice and at Cologne, in 1616, by Hierat,
with some additional matter. This Cologne edition
of 1616 is the one from which the translations have
been made for the present work, and to which the
references in it as to volume, page and letter refer. The
ten folio volumes are usually, as in the author's copy,
bound in six. Had the present book been a critical one,

recourse must, of course, have been had to the Bene-
dictine edition; but for the purpose for which he
writes, the author considered that his reprint of the
Louvain text would be sufficiently accurate; his object
being not to determine or explain any particular
reading in S. Augustine, but to supply his brother
priests with a few sermon thoughts which were
suggested by the words of this great Doctor of the
Western Church. Should "Augustine the Preacher"
meet with a fair amount of success, it will be followed
at no very distant interval by a like volume upon
Origen, treated after the same plan.

J. M. A.

Laus Deo.

INDEX OF SERMONS.

SERMON I.

THE PLURALITY OF SIN.

" Death reigned by one."—*Rom.* v. 17.

S. Augustine.—" In that one sin which by one
man entered into the world, and passed upon all
men—on account of which little children also are baptized—many sins can be understood, if the one itself
be divided into its several members. For pride also is
here, since man chose to be in his own power rather
than in that of God ; and sacrilege, because he did
not believe in God ; and homicide, because he cast
himself into death ; and spiritual fornication, because
the integrity of the human mind was corrupted by the
persuasion of a serpent ; and theft, because he used
forbidden food ; and covetousness, because he desired
more than ought to have satisfied him ; and if any
other in this one admitted sin can be found by diligent consideration."—*Ench. ad Lau.* c. xlv. vol. iii.
p. 64, F.

At first sight, it seems as if the punishment which
God inflicted upon the human race on account of the

B

sin of Adam, was too stringent and severe. It appears to be out of proportion, that death for all time should flow down upon the human race for one single act of disobedience which was committed so many thousands of years ago. Yet, on further consideration, it is evident that the first single act of disobedience was not a simple one; that it involved many other sins in its commission. An investigation of the transgression of Adam, leads to the clear conviction and understanding of the fact : that no act of sin can be simple or single; that there is a plurality of sin in every sinful thought, word, or deed. When any sin is thoroughly sifted and examined, it is found to be made up of many factors. The sin of Adam—an act of disobedience—contains within it the several sins of—

I. *Pride.*—Adam wanted to be in his own power; to be his own master; to be as a God, intellectually cognisant of good and evil. He hitherto had been passive in God's hands, now he desired to act and think for himself. His pride of heart rose up against any entire submission to the will of God. This pride led the creature to exalt itself against the Creator. Pride is at the root of all disobedience; obedience is ever humble.

II. *Sacrilege.*—It was a robbery of God arising from having robbed Him of faith and love. A sacrilegious spirit is very common; it despoils God of

much that belongs to Him ; it is a violation or pro-
fanation of sacred things. The body and soul of the
baptized are consecrated to God, so that every post-
baptismal sin is an act of sacrilege. Our bodies are
temples of the Holy Ghost. "If any man defile the
temple of God him shall God destroy." (1 Cor. iii.
17.) Every sin becomes, therefore, sacrilege ; that
is, a violation of grace, knowledge, and of the powers
which belong to God.

III. *Homicide.*—Man was created deathless, and
the "Tree of Life" was planted as a further security
against any kind of death. Adam had heard that the
punishment of disobedience was death. All disobedience is a slaying of that higher spiritual nature which
is our true and very selves. A man is a homicide
who slays his soul by sin, quenching in it all the
action of grace, and stilling its every impulse towards
the higher life. The death that such an homicide
entails upon its victim, is eternal, and one full of agony
and woe.

IV. *Covetousness.*—Adam seemed to have everything that man could want ; all things in heaven and
earth were given to him to be his portion, and yet he
was not satisfied. The covetous never feel that they
can gain enough ; they are ever murmuring against
God's providence, and trying to overreach His ordering
of things. Contentment and obedience go hand in hand.

Epilogue.—Sin cannot stand alone.   It is—1) the result of many unholy influences ; 2) a beginning that carries a long procession of other sins in its train. 3) Hence sin is only an act in its manifestation ; it is in its nature a combination and a principle.

SERMON II.

THE ATTEMPTS OF SATAN.

"Satan hindered us."—1 *Thess.* ii. 18.

S. Augustine.—"We should observe 'the head' (Gen. iii. 15) of Satan, for he observes 'the heal' not of our feet, but the end of the mind, so that he can by any means retain upon earthly things by his bite, the mind running towards things heavenly."—*Ser.* lxxvi. *ad Frat. Erem.* vol. x. p. 674, B.

"There is much need to judge and to discern; since Satan transfigures himself into an angel of light; lest by deceiving he seduces into something evil; for when the sense of body deceives, the mind indeed is not moved from the opinion which is true and right, by which every one leads a faithful life, and there is no danger to religion. Or when he feigns himself to be good, or says or does those things which pertain to the good angels, even if he is believed to be good, there is no error either dangerous or morbid to the Christian faith. But when by means of these external things he begins to lead to his own things, then it becomes a great and a necessary vigilance to discern, and not to follow him."—*Ench. ad Lau.* c. li. vol. iii. p. 66, D.

Not S. Paul alone, but all who desire to become more holy and obedient, more like Jesus Christ, are "hindered" by Satan. He tries to delay repentance ; to stay contrition; to drown good resolutions ; to quench the promptings of God the Holy Ghost within. He spares no pains, no labour, no craft to keep the soul from God. He hinders every advance in the Christian life by raising up discouragements such as—

I. *Doubts.*—Where there is any doubt, our lowly nature is but too ready to construe it its own way. Thousands of souls have been lost by a doubt. If we doubt about—1) Sacrament grace, what need to seek the Sacrament ? about—2) Holy Scripture, what need to study it, or to seek to order our lives by it ? 3) Heaven and eternity, why should we so discipline ourselves as to be worthy of an entrance there ? 4) Hell and the Last Judgment : what terrors have the place of the lost and last judgment for our souls ? To the doubting soul, the future life, promise and threat are all alike. Satan loves a doubt.

II. *Difficulties.*— The conquest of difficulties makes up the sum of any life that is worth the living for. The disciplinal life on earth is rightly intended by God to be one long unending contest with difficulty. The life of holiness, because its reward is so great, and its satisfaction so keen, is necessarily a very difficult life to lead. It is most difficult—1) to break through old-established habits of sin. Custom in all things is second nature; in sin it may be said to be nature itself. 2) To rise from the dead level of worldliness on the wings of faith, towards higher and better things. 3) To overcome the pleadings and instincts of our old nature. All these difficulties are a great delight to Satan, if by them he can stay the Christian's course.

III. *Distractions.*—Satan hates a concentrated, vigorous purpose. He delights to break up the mind, and so dissipate and weaken its powers. He strives to distract the soul from—1) earnest thought; 2) reading and meditation; 3) prayer. This he does by ever intruding—1) worldly thoughts in holy places and seasons; 2) cares, when the soul seeks rest with God; 3) temptations, when the Spirit is pleading with the conscience for holiness.

Epilogue.—"All things are possible to him that believeth. The question is, Shall we allow Satan to hinder us? Is he our master, or is he not? If not, is God not stronger than he? Shall he ruin me both in body and in soul whilst I can help myself? What are his doubts, difficulties, and distractions, if I seek

to run with patience the race towards heaven which is
set before me, looking unto Jesus? His blessed presence scatters them all to the winds. A most vain
excuse "I wanted to be pure and holy, but 'Satan
hindered me.'" No, rather I feel that "I can do all
things through Christ Who strengtheneth me."

SERMON III.

THE MOUNTAINS OF ISRAEL.

"I will feed them upon the mountains of Israel."—*Ezek.* xxxiv. 13.

S. Augustine.—"He appointed 'the mountains of Israel,' the Authors of the divine Scriptures. Feed ye there, that ye may feed securely. Whatsoever ye may have thence heard, let it savour well to you; reject whatsoever is without, lest ye wander in fog. Hear ye the voice of your Shepherd; gather ye yourselves together to the mountains of Holy Scripture. There, are delights for your heart; there, is nothing poisonous, nothing foreign; they are most fertile pastures; only come ye, and be ye fed upon the mountains of Israel."—*De Pastor.* c. xi. vol. ix. p. 246, E.

As our Blessed Lord did afterwards, so did the Prophet, speaking nearly five hundred and ninety years before He came, use the outward world of nature to represent the inward world of grace; speaking prophetically of that Good Shepherd hereafter to come Who would spiritually feed His flock in those fruitful, joyous, free, and open pastures, in which there would be food enough and to spare, and all the joyousness of combined holiness and knowledge.

Holy Scripture is then well likened to the " mountains of Israel," inasmuch as it is—

I. *Pleasant.*—" There are delights for your heart." A glorious feeling to roam upon the mountain-sides, treading the soft herbage under foot; inhaling the light pure air; catching the expanse and view which seems to lead the soul onward towards those eternal realms in which the sun is ever shining, and where sin, sorrow, and death never come. In Holy Scripture, as upon the mountain-top—1) we breathe a purer air than belongs to this common world and life. The motives and principles which it sets before us are so noble, high, and pure, that it takes us for a time away from and above all the low, paltry, and petty feelings and interests which so lower and mar the beauty of our daily lives. We are nourished by an air so light and hopeful, so untainted by the bitterness of the spirit of man. 2) Upon the mountain, how expansive is the vision, the gentle slopes beneath our feet; the valleys stretching far away; the distant hills all blue with sun and mist, faint emblems of God's Holy City. Holy Scripture is the earliest record of man's race; it begins with the creation of the world. Embracing all the past, it includes all the present; it reaches onward by its prophecy to that new heaven and new earth, in which for ever the glorified shall tarry around the throne of the Lamb. 3) How free, too, is it on the hills; room for every action; all that cramps and hinders bodily development is far removed. Holy Scripture frees the soul from the bonds of superstition, fear, and doubt, giving a new liberty as well as a new life to the spirit, by which it becomes free indeed.

II. *Harmless.*—"There is nothing poisonous" or harmful, upon the mountains. Over those rounded hillocks of Israel, there lurk no secret dangers, no hidden enemies; life on them is as safe as it is innocent. No secret sources of harm, no tinge of that which ought not to be, can be found in Holy Scripture. For—1) it is perfect because inspired. There is always a danger to be apprehended when the mind unduly feeds upon the imperfect works of man. The highest profane writer, a Plato, or a Shakespeare, leaves some traces of his own dark spots upon the earnest student. 2) It is infallible, it cannot err; it can never lead astray its followers. The best human systems contain some mistake or error in them, which it would be deadly to embrace.

III. *Personal.*—" There is nothing foreign," standing upon the mountain; there is a feeling, " I am monarch of all I survey:" it belongs to me. A sense of personal possession accompanies such a position. Holy Scripture, the more it is known, loved, and

studied, becomes the soul's very own.   1) It supplies
the wants of the inward man ; 2) it appeals to the
deeper feelings of man's highest and best nature ; 3)
it enters into and sympathises with all the emotions
of our Godlike nature.   Holy Scripture is nothing, if
it does not satisfy the mind, develope the affections,
and sympathize with man's joys and sorrows.

IV. *Fruitful.*—" They are most fertile pastures."
The " hills drop fatness," fragrant with grass and sweet
herbs ; so is Holy Scripture most fruitful in—1) examples to be followed and avoided ; 2) warnings ; 3)
promises to encourage and to comfort.

Epilogue.—Feed, then, upon those mountains—1)
daily—2) prayerfully—3) reflectively.

SERMON IV.

THE CHRISTIAN PREACHER.

"Though I taught them, rising up early and teaching them, yet they have not hearkened to receive instruction."—*Jer.* xxxii. 33.

S. Augustine.—" They who learn are Christians; they who hear and do not learn—what are they to the sower? The path does not scare the hand of the sower; the stones and thorns do not frighten him. The sower throws around that which is his own. He who fears lest his seed should fall into bad ground, will not gain the good soil. And we speak, we scatter seed, we cast forth the grain, and there are those who slight, who censure, who ridicule. If we feared such, we should have nothing sown; and at the season of harvest nothing to eat. Therefore may the seed fall upon good ground. I know that he who hears, and hears well, both fails and profits. He fails in iniquity, he profits in the truth; he fails for this world, he profits towards God."—*De Discip. Christ.* c. xiii. vol. ix. p. 276, D.

The preacher asks with saddened voice, How many are Christians? How many are they who learn?

What is the number of those who slight, condemn, and ridicule his holy message ? The answer to these questions often weighs his soul down with sorrow ; he utters, in heartbroken accents, the complaint of Jeremiah, " Though I taught them," etc. He longs to close his mouth for ever, yet he thinks of the season of the harvest—of the harvest of souls, and of the fearful state of having at that time " nothing to eat," no fruit to show, for all his prayer and toil and travail, in the vineyard of the Lord. That the Christian preacher may, without hopelessness, hold on his course —never waxing faint in energy and courage—he must remember that his work is—

I. *Hidden.*—A delight in all work in which the effect is immediate and manifest. The skill of the physician cures the disease very soon and perceptibly ; all men can see the cure. It is so also with the producer, the painter, the sculptor, the artificer. The Preacher's work is a hidden work ; it deals with souls rather than with bodies—with spirit rather than with matter. It appeals to feelings which are amongst the most sacred and the most secret of our being. God, Who alone judgeth the heart, can see the work of the preacher. Men often feel acutely, are moved to the very depths, and yet they give no sign. The seed is really sown, albeit it is hidden in the ground : the snow and frost are overlying it, yet still it is there.

So is the word hidden in the soil of the soul, covered with the snow of conventionality, and the frost of the habit of indifference; abiding there in secret for its work to be made manifest in due time. Preaching is a work of faith : as such it is necessarily a hidden work; hidden in—1) its beginnings ; 2) its operations ; 3) its results.

II. *Gradual.*—As a rule the word sinks into the soul like the leaven into the dough which it leavens by slow degrees. Our words seem to fall powerless and unheeded, all the time they are slowly " converting the soul." The greatest effects—like the physical changes on the surface of the earth—lose their marvel when they are slowly produced. The gradual change which may be going on before our very eyes is often wholly unnoticed by us.

III. *Contested.*—The work of the preacher is fought against—1) by his own infirmities and sins; 2) by the world without, which he denounces; 3) by the world of sin within, which he detects and exposes. All these things are against us—the world, the flesh, and the devil with his wiles.

IV. *Eternal.*—The work of the preacher is for eternity and not for time. To eternity is relegated its—1) reward ; 2) issues; 3) manifestation. The true preacher looks beyond the present time and life; he dies leaving his mission largely unfulfilled ; yet at the resurrection of the just, will he be blest, and all his labour fully rewarded.

Epilogue.—Let the preacher learn well, then, the threefold lesson of—1) patience; 2) hope; 3) courage.

SERMON V.

DEATH A SEPARATION.

"The Spirit shall return unto the God Who gave it."—
Eccles. xii. 7.

S. Augustine.—" Wherefore that which pertains to the death of the body—that is the separation of the mind from the body, since they who suffer it are called the dying—is good for no one. For the force itself by which the two are torn asunder has a harsh feeling [asperum sensum] and one contrary to nature, since both had been joined together and interwoven in the living subject until it may die ; until all the feeling may be taken away which was introduced by the entrance of mind and flesh. Which entire trouble sometimes one stroke of the body, or one seizure of the mind stops ; nor is it even permitted to be felt, coming so quickly."—*De Civit. Dei, lib.* xiii. c. 6, vol. v. p. 139, B.C.

The world is full of wonderful separations ; but that which takes place between the body and the soul is the most wonderful of them all. Since we shall all have to pass through the grave and the gate of death, we cannot be too prepared for this most wonderful and mysterious change. As an event so certain, and often so sudden, a few thoughts about it can never be unacceptable and out of place. Death comes before the mind in many aspects; but the special one to be considered now, is a separation between the body and the soul; the body will return to the earth and see corruption, and " the spirit shall return unto the God Who gave it." We note therefore, that—

I. *There is something to be separated.*—Life, whatever it may be, grows with the body and ends with it. There is in man a something united with this physical or animal life, yet above it and distinct from it, which is called " spirit," or the immortal part of our nature. In this " spirit of a man " dwells the reason, the memory, the will, and the affections. This spirit leads a life of its own ; in part independent of the body. It is capable of cultivation; it has its hopes, fears, joys and sorrows quite independently of the body. When the animal life is brought by disease to its lowest ebb, the spiritual life, not unrarely, is found to be at its flood and spring. The highest form of life is manifested when the spirit, or mind, and the body are united; working together in harmony and strength. " A sound mind in a sound body," according to the old saw. Revelation, philosophy, and reason

all combine to bear their several testimonies to the
" mind " or " spirit " which exists in man. It is the
possession of this which makes man—1) Godlike;
2) Progressive; 3) Deathless.

II. *Death is this separation.*—Death is the "return
of the spirit to God Who gave it;" the taking of the
spirit, and the leaving of the body. Hence death is
—1) The breaking up of an old union. Mind and
body may have lived together for many a year; have
mutually given and received much the one from the
other. The body too, has both educated and
disciplined the mind, which has gained its manifold
knowledge and experience through the senses of the
body. Yes! the body may have been at times
a hard master, overbearing, if not kept in due
subjection, but at no time has it been an uncareful
one. So, through weal or woe, in sickness and
in health, these two companions have journeyed on
together, and now they are going to part company.
2) Death is also a change of state; not a higher,
but a lower state. The " unclothed " state (2 Cor.
v. 4.) is not one of the highest honour. At death,
however, free from all impediment, the spirit returns
"unto the God Who gave it," and the body goes down
to the silent grave. A state this of wonderful life for
the one; of corruption for the other.

How do they part company? No one from the

spirit-world has returned to answer this question.   S.
Augustine says with " a harsh feeling."   Others say
that the last sigh is one of pleasure, not of pain ; that
death is but the opening of the prison doors, through
which the disembodied soul, joyfully and eagerly wings
her flight ; all signs of sorrow and weakness being for
ever over with her.   This may be so.   God grant, that
although death is the punishment of sin, yet that it
may be no unpleasant thing to die.

III. *This separation or death is only for a limited
time.*—Mortality will one day be " swallowed up of
life."   Not for ever is the body to remain in the grave ;
not for ever is the soul to abide in Paradise.   The
separation, called death, will be cancelled by and at
a reunion, which is called " the resurrection of the
dead."   This separation, is then, a prelude to a union ;
to another life which will be—1) Immortal, as never
to end ; 2) Eternal, as no longer subject to change ;
3) Glorious, as shining with the purity and holiness
of the City of God.   Death is truly the " corn of wheat
cast into the ground," which bringeth forth much
fruit, after many days ; which fruit consists in the
uniting of body and spirit more closely and enduringly
than ever they were before knit together.

Epilogue.—Such then is death, since Jesus Christ
by His death took away the sting of death ; and by
His rising from the dead ; for the very body even

changed death into a sleep. Not now to speak of the unholy dead : only remember that if you would die the death of Jesus Christ, if you would sleep in Him, you must live His life.

SERMON VI.

THE TREE OF LIFE.

" The tree of life also in the midst of the garden."—*Gen.* ii. 9.

S. Augustine.—" The tree of life planted in the midst of Paradise signifies that wisdom by which the mind ought to understand that it is ordered in a certain middle state: that although it holds all bodily nature in subjection to it, yet it considers that the nature of God is above it, and that neither may it decline to the right hand by arrogating to itself that which does not belong to it, nor to the left, by despising, through carelessness, that which it is. This is ' the Tree of Life,' planted in the middle of Paradise." —*De Gen. C. Man. lib.* ii. c. 9, vol. i. p. 318, E.

We suffer many a sorrow and commit many a sin by being untrue to ourselves; by our not remembering sufficiently that " middle state " to which our spiritual and higher nature belongs; by our not partaking of that " Tree of Life," of which the fruit is that true and heavenly wisdom which reveals to us that which we are, as well as tells us that which we are not. We all need—

I. *A holy and lawful pride.*—Pride in its true
sense is an attribute given by God. It is absolutely
essential for the maintenance of due and proper self-
respect. When we lose an honest pride in ourselves
and our belongings, we lose the respect of ourselves,
of others, and of God. Jesus Christ came on earth
to dwell in the Paradise of the soul : to be "unto us
wisdom" (1 Cor. i. 30), our very "Tree of Life;"
teaching us a full and true knowledge of ourselves,
lest we should be unduly swallowed up of sorrow, or
by the sense of our own weakness, and of our shame.
The true pride of the regenerate man consists in his
mind, which ought to hold all bodily nature in subjection as being superior to it in—1) Immortality.
Death, or non-existence, for a time hath passed upon
the body. The mind hath never forfeited its life and
being. Whilst the "outward man," at a certain age,
must decay day by day, the mind may be gaining fresh
power during all this time. 2) Progress, which soon
reaches a definite and impassable line in the "bodily
nature," but in which the mind knows no let or hindrance
in its journey towards perfection. This unlimited capacity is the great glory of the spirit of man. 3) Victory,
for the mind is able to triumph over all pain and
bodily infirmity, over the ghostly enemy of the body,
death itself ; over all the pleadings of the flesh ; over
all the bodily senses. That "they who are Christ's

have crucified the flesh, with its affections and lusts."
4) Holiness, or the likeness to God. The bodily
nature must ever remain the same. The Ethiopian
can never change his skin, but grace can and does
change the heart, and forms it anew after the image
and likeness of God. A lawful pride for the spirit of
man, when it feels that it is united with the Spirit of
God; a pride which should stay the mind from all
that is unworthy or degrading. Hence the " Tree
of Life," or of wisdom, teaches man a true and holy
pride.

II. *A due Humility.*—Wisdom, the Tree of Life,
teaches my soul that " the nature of God is above it,"
and immeasurably superior to it, for the soul of man
s —1) created. God its Creator is Incarnate; it is
but a creature, owing its life and being to Him.
Inconceivable distance between the Creator and the
creature. 2) Limited in power and knowledge; not
omnipresent, omnipotent, and omniscient. 3) Insufficient for itself, it must lean upon something
beyond itself, and can only be really satisfied and
happy when it leans upon God. 4) Dependent wholly
upon God, in Him it lives, moves, and has its being.
The more and the better the mind knows itself, the
more does it blush for its own weaknesses and imperfections. Hence " the Tree of Life," or of Wisdom,
teaches us a true humility.

III. *A strict self-discipline.*—Heavenly wisdom, our Tree of Life, warns against declining to the right hand or to the left; not living a middle life between an unholy pride and a craven humility, remembering that "The mind created by the Highest Good is a great good, but not the Highest Good; the flesh is neither the highest good, nor a great good, but a small one. The mind, then, is a great good, but not the highest good; living between the Highest Good and the small good; that is, between God and the flesh; inferior to God, superior to the flesh." (*S. Aug. De Verb. Apost. Ser.* xiii. c. 6.) Hence the lessons must be learned of—1) Moderation; 2) Circumspection; 3) Forethought in the conduct of life; that the golden means may be found out, and ever be exercised.

Epilogue.—This "Tree of Life" teaches us the lessons of discipline and a right walk. Man has the power of reaching, by grace, to God; of sinking, if he will to do so, to hell. Life and being are indeed a fearful trust and responsibility.

SERMON VII.

TYPES OF THE CHURCH.

"She shall be brought unto the King in raiment of needlework."—
Ps. xlv. 14.

S. Augustine.—" The Church is that Queen concerning whom the Lord spake these words. For She is the Mother of all believers, who regenerates to salvation those who are born to death; called, indeed, after the Synagogue, but promised before it."—*Ser. De Temp.* ccliii. vol. x. p. 261, A.

Let us follow S. Augustine, and note some few of the types of the Church which are to be found in Holy Scriptures.

I. *Eve.*—" The Church was prefigured by the first man; for as Eve was formed from the side of Adam, so the redeemed Church sprang from the body and the wound of Christ."—*Ser. De Temp.* ccliii. vol. x. p. 261, A.

Hence the Church is—1) Human, bound up with every human hope and sympathy; 2) Divine, as formed by grace and not by nature, an emblem of our own new life

II. *Abel and Seth.*—"In holy Abel was the Catholic Church."—*Ser. De Temp.* ccxvi. vol. x. p. 323, C.

"From these two men, Abel, which is interpreted 'weeping,' and Seth, which signifies 'resurrection,' is prefigured the death of Christ and His life from the dead; from which belief is produced this City of God."—*De Civit. Dei, lib.* xv. c. 18, vol. v. p. 168, D.

The very existence of the Church proclaims—1) a death unto sin of the old man; 2) a rising again to newness of life.

III. *The Ark of Noah.*—"A deluge was at one time made over the whole earth, that sinners might be blotted out, and yet they who escaped from it in the Ark pointed out the Sacrament of the Church of the future which now swims over the billows of the world, and yet is saved from submersion by the wood of the Cross of Christ."—*De Catec. Rud.* c. 27, vol iv. p. 272, G.

"Without doubt it [the Ark] is a figure of the City of God—that is, the Church—sojourning in this world, which is saved by the wood upon which Christ hung, the One Mediator between God and man, the Man Christ Jesus."— *De Civit. Dei, lib.* xvi. c. 26, vol. v. p. 172, C.

Hence the Church is a place of—1) Refuge; 2) of need, since all salvation hangs upon it.

IV. *Jerusalem.*—"This Jerusalem, Holy Church, the Spouse of Christ in the Apocalypse of S. John is copiously and faithfully described."—*C. Faust. lib.* xv. c. 10, vol. vi. p. 114, B.

Hence the Church is—1) Glorious, the City of the great King; 2) Free. "The Jerusalem which is above is free." (Gal. iv. 26.) 3) Holy. "There shall enter into it nothing that defileth." (Rev. xxii. 15.)

V. *The Fleece of Gideon.*—"The grace of the One Mediator between God and man was lying hidden in the people of God, but as if in a moist fleece. (Judges vi. 38.) But now, as if that fleece being dry, that is, the Jewish people being reprobated, amongst all nations it is discerned as if exposed upon a threshing-floor."—*Cont. Pel. and Cel.* c. 25, vol. vii. p. 303, C.

This similitude points to an inward and an outward grace in the Church. In former times, this grace was —1) limited in distinction; 2) unknown to men; 3) inoperative. When the fleece was squeezed dry, then it became—1) unlimited in its application; 2) known to all men; 3) full of might and power. In the heart, as in the Church, there often exists large measures of grace and resource. The soul is a moist fleece indeed, but until it is pressed by sorrow, tried, or occasions the inmost grace and resource, is not known or manifested in results. The Church has an inward as well as an outward presence.

VI. *Hannah.*—" Hannah, also the mother of Samuel, who at first was barren, and afterwards was rejoiced by becoming fruitful; when exulting she poured out her thanksgiving to God, is seen to prophesy nothing else than this [the City of God]. Hannah is interpreted 'his grace,' the Christian religion itself; the City of God itself, of which Christ is the Founder."—*De Civ. Dei, lib.* xvii. c. 4, vol. v. 192.

The Church is not merely a mediator and an instructor, but a mother also; who by regeneration brings forth sons and daughters to God.

VI. *The undefiled Dove.*—(*Cant.* vi. 9; *Eph.* v. 27.) "' For she is without spot and wrinkle :' so the Apostle affirms that they alone are able to be members of this dove who have renounced the world in words though not in deeds."—*De Baptis. lib.* iv. c. iii. vol. vii. p. 46, D.

" That dove bewailing wickedness among many crows."—*De. Bapt. lib.* v. c. 16, vol. vii. p. 56, G.

This type indicates the Church Militant to be a school of holiness, in which the soul is to be prepared for the society of the holy in the Church Triumphant. Holiness is to be specially obtained in the Church by means of—1) Prayer; 2) Sacraments; 3) Instruction.

Epilogue.—Sin is many-sided, grace is many-sided,

and so the Church, who is the manifestation of grace is many-sided too. The Church adapts herself to the infinite wants of man with the one object of leading many sons and daughters to glory.

SERMON VIII.

MEMORY.

"When my soul fainted within me, I remembered the Lord."—
Jonah ii. 7.

S. Augustine.—" Memory is the consort of, and
co-worker with, reason, since without it, reason could
neither proceed to the unknown, nor retain any know-
legde of that which is known. Memory is the power
which the soul has of retaining things received; of
reproducing the past; of recollecting that which has
glided away."—*De Spirit. et Ani.* c. xxxvi. vol. iii
p. 366, G.

" Memory is the power by which the mind recalls
those things which have been."—*Octogint. Quæst.*
q. xxvi. vol iv. p. 204, F.

" I beseech you, brethren, not to hear purposelessly;
but to hold these things, to ruminate, and hence to
feed upon them. The memory is to man, what the
stomach is to cattle. The unclean beasts do not
ruminate. (Deut. xiv. 6,7.) Rumination appertains to
those who muse afterwards upon what they have
heard."—*Hom.* xxxv. tom. x. p. 168, D.

"I come next into the spacious fields and vast palaces of memory; where are treasured up numberless forms and images. There all these things are kept distinctly and by their several kinds. There, heaven, earth, and sea are presented to me. There also I meet with myself and take a review of myself, what I have done, when and where and how I was influenced when I did it. Great is the power of the memory, exceeding great, O my God; an inward room, spacious and boundless: who can sound the bottom of it? And this is a power of my soul and belongs to my nature, and I myself am not able to comprehend all that I myself am."—*Confers. lib.* x. c. 8.

It is memory that colours our every thought, word, and action. This great power of the soul is indeed—

I. *The Child of the Past.*—It is an old speculation, that all knowledge is but reminiscence, the shadows cast from a former time. The memory of the past presents us with a mingled reflection of—1) Joys, long since departed; of friends and scenes that can return no more; of hopes unfulfilled. By the action of memory, just once again the early brightness of our springtime becomes our own. 2) Sorrows, that formed marked phases in our lives; past agonies, from

which may it please God to keep us for the future.
3) Sins, trials, and temptations, over which we fought
and wrestled to our utmost. A beautiful Christmas
story was founded upon the text—" Lord, keep my
memory green."

II. *The Sister of the Present.*—Almost impossible
to order life, if there were no experience by which we
could be guided. Experience is the action of memory
upon the present; since experience—1) Directs the
choice or selection in things which are doubtful or
difficult; 2) supports, under any special trouble or
sorrow; 3) gives a wisdom which is all its own. It
has rubbed off many a prejudice; rounded many a
corner; and enlarged almost indefinitely the mind's
view of men and things. It is experience which gives
the mature wisdom of age as contrasted with the
rashness and folly of youth.

III. *The Parent of the Future.*—The united
memories of the past tinge the future with their own
particular hue; for whilst memory lasts, the actions
of the past done long since, influence the future for
weal or woe. Rightly applied, memory makes our
future—1) Hopeful; so many mercies of the past bid
us not despair for the future. 2) Humble; such
infinite cause for humility in the manifold trans-
gressions and omissions which rise up in self-con-
demnation against us. 3) Hallowed; by its relation-

D

ship to all that memory points out as having gone before it.

Epilogue.—Dedicate to God this glorious gift of memory ; consecrate it to His service by using it—1) In earnest self-examination ; 2) in prayer for pardon of past sin ; 3) as the ground of a loving and a humble faith.

SERMON IX.

ETERNITY.

"Eternal life."—*Rom.* vi. 23.

S. Augustine.—"The word eternal is understood in two significations, as the 'world without end,' that is, 'ever, without end,' or till we may come to eternity." *Enarr. in Ps.* cxxx. vol. viii. p. 347, G.

"Eternity lacks beginning, needs no addition, has no end, remains without change."—*Sent.* iii. vol. iii. p. 376, D.

"That which is unchangeable is eternal, for it is ever in the same state. But whatsoever is changeable is subject to time, for it is not ever in the same state, and therefore cannot rightly be called eternal. That which is changed does not remain; and that which does not remain is not eternal. Therefore there is a difference between the immortal and the eternal; be cause everything which is eternal is immortal, but not everything which is immortal can exactly be called eternal. If anything should live for ever yet suffer change, it cannot rightly be called eternal, since it

D 2

continues not for ever in the same state, although it can rightly be called immortal since it ever lives. But sometimes it is called eternal because it is immortal. That is properly called eternal when it has no past, as if it had passed on; no future, as if it had not yet attained—but that which it is, it is that alone."— *Octogint. Quæst.* qu., xix. vol. iv. p. 206, A.

" Eternal life," in its highest and truest significance, is a changeless life; a condition of absolute and perfect rest. If deathlessness could be granted to us in this world, how wretched should we be. The myth of Tithonus shows how miserable would be immortality without eternity; how absolutely terrible it would be to be subject to change and decay, and yet not to be able to die. The immortal life in heaven does not consist merely in living on, but in living a changeless, that is, an eternal life.

This eternity or unchangeableness can be considered in relation to—

I. *State.*—Here we are ever changing. The habits of our bodies; our tastes, our pursuits; our very dwelling-places; and each and every change is like turning over some new page in the book of life; it is a fresh beginning; it gathers around it a new cluster of associations. If there were absolutely no changes in this world, life would be wearisomely monotonous, and this because it is an imperfect life and state; but when it is perfect—then the changeless state would in itself be an eternity of bliss. The eternal state is perfect in respect of—1) Life; 2) Happiness; 3) Glory.

II. *Employment.*—One eternal employment in the deathless life; one of which the soul will never tire because it cannot do so. This employment will consist in—1) Loving God, with all the fulness of the renewed affections; 2) Praising Him with all the power of the soul; 3) Serving Him with every energy of a strengthened and purified will. Eternal love and praise and service will form the employment of eternal blessedness "for ever and ever."

III. *Companionship.*—The ties of heaven unlike the ties of earth will last for ever; no weariness amongst the mutual company of that throng of redeemed men and angelic natures. Eternal, and because eternal, they will be unchangeable in their fellowship, having a common—1) Interest; the joy of one will be the joy of all. 2) Nature; subject to like conditions of existence, all being ' children of the Most Highest.' 3) Service; the King of kings and Lord of lords.

Epilogue.—Our Blessed Lord became Incarnate not only to render this " eternal life " possible to us—to procure for us this changeless immortality of bliss—

but to show us how it may, nay must, become our state when we die. "Eternal life" is in this twofold sense, "through Jesus Christ our Lord." We are bound to love and follow Jesus Christ living as eternal ones, as far as may be; casting the shadow of immortality over all our footsteps. Then shall death be neither a separation or a change, but the completion of the present state, service, and companionship.

SERMON X.

THE PREACHER OF THE WORLD.

" Never man spake like this man."—*S. John* vii. 46.

S. Augustine.—" The Preacher of the world, from a certain watch-tower of high authority, cries aloud : ' Hear, O human race ! hearken, O ye sons of Adam ! listen, O ye people, laborious and unfruitful !' "—*De Verb. Apost. Ser.* xxii. vol. x. p. 126, A.

The " Preacher of the world " is a true and noble title for our Blessed Lord whilst He was on earth. The world has known some few great preachers and teachers between Noah and Socrates—earnest, noble, prophetic souls, in whom were hearts throbbing with the pulse of humanity—men who fulfilled a noble mission during life, and a still nobler mission when they died. Despite their greatness and their goodness, they were but preachers, speaking in their own name, to the immediate age in which they lived ; to certain classes only of their fellow-men. Jesus Christ stands out alone, as being not only a, but " *the* Preacher of the World," Whose preaching has three notes or marks which are essentially peculiar to it. The "Preacher of the World" preached—

I. *With authority.*—All human preaching must be tinged with many a doubtful thought or expression; it must partake in some degree of that error and infirmity which is ever present with all human thoughts, words, and works. The "Preacher of the world" taught with authority (S. Matt. vii. 29) and not as the Scribes. There was nothing tentative or speculative in His teaching; it conveyed the assured message of one who was fully invested with power to deliver it. The authority flowed—1) From the "Preacher of the World" Himself: He was divine as well as human. In His case it was not merely a fallible yet earnest man pleading with his fellows; it was the infallible Word of God—the Creator and the future Redeemer of the world, in Whom were hid "all the treasures of wisdom and knowledge"—it was the very "Way, the Truth, and the Life," in bodily form proclaiming Himself. 2) The divine authority of the message: "As My Father hath taught Me, I speak these things." (S. John viii. 28.) It was a message of God, delivered from God to man by the mouth of the Lord Jesus Christ; for "the Lord hath spoken" a message by which man was to be an infinite gainer. 3) Supported by the divine testimony of miracles: the Word was confirmed by many miracles, by signs and wonders such as alone could come from God. The Preacher of the World was authoritative in His Person, message, and testimonies.

II. *For all time.*—All merely human teachings and preachings are only of value, or of primary value, at least, when they were first delivered. Their chief relationship was with existent circumstances, which soon pass away. The difficulties and troubles of their day are not the doubts and difficulties of our day. Hence all such preaching, after a certain time, loses its full force and significance. From the Incarnation to the end of the world, the relationship between God and man will remain inviolate; hence the preaching of the Lord sounds as fresh in our ears now as it did to the men who heard Him in the flesh eighteen hundred years ago. His words, His discourses, and His parables apply not to one age alone, they are for all time; as fresh and to the purpose now as they ever were. " The Preacher of the World " embraces in His preaching—1) The past, the present, and the future; 2) the fulness of the unchangeable mind of God; 3) the unalterable conditions of sin and weakness which are attached to man so long as he is in this present life.

III. *For all estates and conditions of men.*—" The Preacher of the World" was not a preacher for a class. His words come home alike to rich and poor, learned and ignorant, holy and profane ; to those in joy, and those in sorrow. Hence His preaching was thoroughly and essentially catholic. It is capable of melting all hearts ; being—1) Earnest, almost to fearlessness. His Life, Words, and Passion, seemed to be all one. 2) Simple, in expression, yet capable of an indefinite expansion of meaning. 3) Loving, so as to draw souls by the bands of love.

Epilogue.—He through His ministers is preaching now. How do His words fall upon the souls that hear.

SERMON XI.

THE BURDENS OF LIFE.

"Bear ye one another's burdens, and so fulfil the Law of Christ."
—*Gal.* vi. 2.

S. Augustine.—" If ' every man shall bear his own
burden' (Gal. vi. 5) how can He say, ' Bear ye one
another's burdens,' unless these burdens are to be
distinguished, or we deem that the Apostle contra-
dicted himself? For not afar off, not in another
epistle, not even in the same epistle either much
before or after this, but in the same place, so that
they are adjoining words he places both these commands, and because each one will have to bear his
own burden, he admonished and exhorted us to bear
one another's burdens. There are therefore some
burdens which each carries for himself; he neither
bears it with another nor casts it upon another. There
are other burdens, concerning which you can rightly
say to a brother, ' I bear it with you,' or ' I bear it
for you.' Against those who were thinking that a
man could be defiled by another's sins, the Apostle

asserted 'every man shall bear his own burden.' On the other hand, against those whom negligence might affect, as being themselves secure that they would not be defiled by other's sins, and so should take no trouble to bear any one else, the Apostle says: ' Bear ye one another's burdens.' It is briefly spoken of and briefly distinguished, and, as far as I can judge, this brevity does not hinder the manifestation of the truth. The burdens which each man bears are his own sins." —*De Verb. Apost. Ser.* xxi. vol. x. p. 223, G.

The seeming paradox that we are both commanded to bear one another's burdens, and every man to bear his own burden, is explained when the difference between the burdens is allowed for. These "burdens" resolve themselves into three classes: those which have to be—

I. *Borne alone.*—Every man has to bear some load which he ever carries with him. It is one great work of sin, that it lays a heavy burden upon the heart and conscience of man. Sin is a load or freight, which the sinner carries with him whithersoever he goes; a load that depresses the spirit and weighs down the mind. Hence when the Apostle says "Every man shall bear his own burden," he makes use of a particular word (*phortion*) to express that burden. The

pardoned sinner has still to carry a certain load of—
1) Remorse and sorrow; not altogether for what he is
now that the sin is forgiven, but for what he might
have been had there been no sin to forgive. Sorrow
for the loss of so much love and grace, health,
strength, time, and opportunity which some special
habit of sin tempted him to either neglect or abuse.
The soul is truly thankful for the Lord's present
mercy and salvation, but not the less will it ever
mourn over a past now beyond recall. 2) Failure, or
disappointment. The early dreams and plans of life
are all unrealized. 'I am not that which I once hoped
to be. I have failed in much that I once thought it
was in my power to accomplish. I have no ground to
attribute this failure to any one but myself, mine was
the failure and mine alone; it is, therefore, my lot to
carry with me through life my sense of it.' 3) Humiliation. A sense of regret and of failure cannot but
bring a feeling of humiliation with it. So humbling
is it to find the ideal life all unrealized; that God's
gifts, whether of nature or of grace, have not produced
their appointed and proper fruit.

II. *Borne with others.*—It is a blessed ordination
of Divine providence that men and women should help
each other as they mutually walk along the pathway
of life. We can all help to bear one another's burdens
by our—1) Sympathy. A joy is only half a joy when

it is locked in the recesses of a single breast. It expands as it becomes shared in by participation. A sorrow is doubly hard to carry when there is no loving ear into which the grief can be poured. Sympathy wonderfully lightens the burden of life. 2) Ministrations of time, knowledge, money, or labour. We all of us have it in our power to render no slight help to others; to bear with them no inconsiderable portion of their burden if we are minded so to do. Woe unto us, if wrapped up in selfishness, the voice of a brother or a sister pleads in vain for help from us. This helping of others and bearing of their burdens with them is, when rightly viewed a—1) Privilege; 2) Responsibility; 3) Most fruitful source of joy to the helper.

III. *Borne for others.*—This is the noblest form of ministration to others; when we bear for them that which they are utterly unable to bear for themselves. Seen—1) on earth in the care bestowed upon the young and the infirm; 2) in heaven in the person of Jesus Christ " Who had borne our griefs and carried our sorrows." Who bids all that "labour and are heavy laden" come to Him. Who suffered, the just for the unjust that He might bring us unto God. He takes my sin upon Himself and gives me holiness; He takes my death and gives me everlasting life. In this respect as in every other He is my great example.

Epilogue.—1) Be careful, not by sin to add "one jot or tittle" more to your own burden. 2) Add not by your example or conduct in any degree to the burdens of others. 3) Seek to enter into another's life, and so abundantly you will be blessed in your own.

SERMON XII.

SOME NOTES OF THE ELECT.

"Bring of the fish which ye have now caught."—S. John xxi. 10.

S. Augustine.—" This is a great mystery in this great Gospel of John. Since there were seven disciples engaged in this fishing, these by their number, seven, signify the end of time. To this period belongs the standing of Jesus on the shore in the morning; for the shore is the end of the sea, and therefore it signifies the end of the world, which is also expressed by Peter who ' drew the net to land.' This the Lord explained in another place (S. Matt. xiii. 48) when the drag-net was cast into the sea, ' So shall it be at the end of the world.' That was a parable, but in this Gospel it is an act, as it will be at the end of the world. The Lord by another fishing signified the Church as she now is. The former fishing He performed at the beginning of His preaching; the latter after His Resurrection; the former capture of fishes signifies both the bad and the good, such as the Church now takes; the latter the good alone which she will hold for ever, complete in the end of the world by the resurrection of the dead. Lastly, Jesus did not there, as here, stand upon the shore. (S. Luke v. 3.) There, the capture of fishes was made in the ships, and not as here did they drag the net to land. By these tokens, by any others which may be noted; there the Church in this world, and here the Church at the end of the world is prefigured : therefore, that fishing was made before, and this one after, the resurrection of the Lord ; for there Christ signified the called, here the raised from the dead. There the nets are not cast on the right side, lest they should signify the good only ; nor on the left side, lest they should signify the bad only; but indifferently He said, ' Let down your nets ' (S. Luke v. 4), that we may understand a mixture of good and evil. Here He said, ' Cast the net on the right side of the ship,' since He would signify those who will stand at the right hand (S. Matt. xxv. 33), the good alone. There on account of the schisms which are signified ' their net brake ;' but here, since in this highest peace of the holy there will be no schisms, it belonged to the Evangelist to relate that ' for all there were so many, yet was not the net broken.' There,

E

was taken "so great a multitude of fishes that both
the ships began to sink," for they were not swamped,
but only in great danger. So is the Church endangered
when her discipline is imperilled by the entrance of a
man with habits wholly alien to the walk of the Saints.
What is the meaning of 'they were not able to draw
it' save that those who pertain to the resurrection of
life, that is to to the right hand; and who enter with
the net of the Christian name, will only appear on
the shore at the end of the world, when they shall
have risen from the dead. Therefore they were not
able to draw the net that they might place in the ship
the fishes which they had taken, as it was done by the
others, by whom the net was broken and the ships
burdened. But the Church holds these right hand
ones, after the end of this life, in a sleep of peace as
in the deep, lying hid until the net comes to the shore
whither it will be drawn. In the former fishing, the
number was not mentioned ; in the latter, the number
of the fishes is 'one hundred and fifty three.' Ten is
the number of the law, the Holy Spirit adds to it
seven, the number of grace ; which number seventeen
makes when multiplied by nine, one hundred and
fifty three. In the first fishing there was 'a great

multitude of fishes,' in the last a definite number of 'great fishes,' for 'whoso shall do and teach My commandments, the same shall be called great in the Kingdom of Heaven.' (S. Matt. v. 19.) And because he will be great here, he will be great there, where ' he that is least ' will find no place."—*Tract in Joan.* cxxii. vol. ix. p. 202, B—H.

Comparing then the two miraculous draughts of fishes with the Parable of the Net (S. Matt. xiii. 47-50), we find three certain notes given to us of the elect; notes by which we can in some degree estimate our own spiritual estate. The finally elect, those who are gathered into the Church triumphant are—

I. *Safe.*—Our baptismal calling and election is well represented by the first miraculous draught of the disciples, when —1) " their net brake " (S. Luke v. 6) and many fishes fell back again into the sea. Alas ! how many baptized Christians fall away from grace. The drag-net of the Church is broken by schism, and the fishes fall away from their " one Lord, one faith, one baptism," from their " first love ;" fall away into —*a*) Superstition ; *b*) Infidelity. In the former case, placing experience before sacrament; the subjective before the objective; and in the latter, giving up all faith, love, and holiness. The net which holds the finally elect stands intact; "and for all there were so

E 2

many, yet was not the net broken." (S. John xxi. 11.)
2) The fishes were but taken into a ship (S. Luke v.
7) which was all but sinking. Full of human infirmity
and imperfection are all earthly dispensations and
conditions. How often the elect soul "begins to
sink" under sorrow, and temptation; the proud
waters have well nigh gone over such a soul to its
destruction. The experience of each member of the
Church Triumphant must be, ' once I began to sink
under my weight of sin, sorrow, trial, and temptation; but now the final shore is reached, the net has
been drawn to land.' (S. John xxi. 11.) Not one
billow more, not one storm, shall ever break over that
devoted head, which is now safely landed on the shore
of Paradise. Let each one strive to make his calling
and election sure, remembering that a state of grace
is alone a state of safety.

II. *Perfect.*—The net of general election is let
down any way, but the net which takes the finally
elect is—1) Let down on the right side of the ship
(S. John xxi. 6), which corresponds to the right hand
of the Judge. (S. Matt. xxv. 33.) The righteous alone
enter into it; they only who love and care for that which
is heavenly and divine. 2) The net was "full of great
fishes," of those good and perfect ones called "great"
as both knowing and doing their Father's will.
(S. Matt. v. 19.) Loving, and desiring, and doing that

which is holy, we shall be found on the right side of the ship, and as " great fishes " and perfect will enter into the joy of the Lord.

III. *Separated.*—At the first draught good and bad were alike taken ; now only the good, which in the parable (S. Matt. xiii. 48) alone are " gathered into vessels." A complete and final separation. Now we must separate from—1) Sinful thoughts ; 2) words ; 3) deeds ; 4) desires. Touch not the unclean thing.

Epilogue.—Seek by holiness of life to become sealed, whilst members of the Church Militant, with this threefold sealing of the elect, which appertains to the Church Triumphant.

SERMON XIII.

THE NEW.

" Behold, I make all things new."—*Rev.* xx 5.

S. Augustine.—" Having assumed manhood, ought He to have created another world that we might believe Him to be the Creator of the world ? But neither a greater world nor one equal to this could be made in this world. Wherefore it was not needful that He should make a new world, but that He should create new things in the world. For a man to be born of a Virgin, raised from the dead to eternal life, and exalted above the heavens, is perhaps a more powerful work than making a world."—*Epist. ad Volu.* vol. ii. p. 6. C.

The pre-incarnate work of Jesus Christ was to make all things of nothing (S. John i. 3), to call into being that which heretofore had not been. The Incarnate work of the Son of God, was to instaurate and renew that which so long ago He had once made. If the former work were the more wonderful, the latter was the more glorious; if the former was more divine, the latter was not less divine but human also. What are these new things which Jesus Christ made in the world? Earth and air and sky; the sun and moon and stars, remain as they were at the beginning. The rainbow now, as then, brings a glory out of storm. Save in the case of the risen body, His " new things " are spiritual, not material; and relate to the world which is invisible rather than to things which can be seen and handled.

Jesus Christ came into this world to give to man—

I. *New Hopes.*—Men were very hopeless just at the time of the Incarnation. The old religions of heathendom were worn out; and the law was swallowed up by and lost in vain traditions; all belief was darkened by a Sadducean spirit. So Jesus Christ came upon earth to give to men—1) A present peace, in which, resting upon Him, the turmoils and pleadings of the heart would be stilled. 2) A future glory and happiness. He came not only to open the Kingdom of Heaven to man, but to bring it in part down to man on earth. He is the " Kingdom of Heaven," and He became in man the hope of glory. It behoveth all who participate in these hopes to purify themselves as He is pure.

II. *New Principles of Action.*—Jesus Christ dissipated the old notions of honour, revenge, and right against might, and numberless like false opinions and practices. The three great principles which He taught, were—1) Love and mercy, as against all the old penal codes. 2) Sincerity in the action of the heart, as well as of the mouth and hand; "Woe unto you, ye hypocrites." 3) Faith, a firm trust and confidence in the higher power and righteous dealings of God.

III. *New Grace and Powers.*—"Grace came by Jesus Christ." (S. John i. 17.) Hence a new power was given to man by means of which he—1) Could overcome sin, "perfecting holiness in the fear of God.' Now the fetters were burst asunder, and the prison doors were thrown wide open. 2) Could in part know and understand God by a new gift of heavenly wisdom. He "was made unto us wisdom and righteousness."

Epilogue.—Jesus Christ hath given to you a new life, new hopes, principles, and powers. Are ye "renewed in the Spirit of your minds?"

SERMON XIV.

OFFERINGS TO GOD.

"None shall appear before Me empty."—*Exod.* xxxiv. 20.

S. Augustine.—"That Zacchæus might come to God, he gave the ' half of his goods' (S. Luke xix. 8); that Peter might come, he relinquished his ship and his nets (S. Matt. iv. 22); that the widow might come, she gave 'two mites' (S. Luke xxi. 2); that one still poorer might come, He held out the ' cup of cold water' (S. Matt. x. 42); that the wholly poor and needy might come, He bestowed goodwill alone. They gave different things, but they came to one Person."—*De Ovib.* c. xvi. vol. ix. p. 256, E.

So provision is made that no one shall come to God without an offering; that the law of Sinai and of Horeb (Deut. xvi. 16) might be fulfilled by Christians till the end of time. The Church of Jesus Christ accepted the law as laid down for her elder sister of Jerusalem (1 Cor. xvi. 2), and in the Primitive Church weekly offerings were made unto God by all His worshippers. Not that God—to Whom all things belong—ever could have any need at the hand of man; but that rather by such offerings, man might render to God "that bounden duty and service" which it becomes a creature, a subject, and a servant to render to his Creator, to his King, and to his Redeemer. For the sake of man, and not for Himself, did God give the command, "None shall appear before Me empty," on this most solemn occasion, by His servant Moses; whilst it was reserved for a great Father of the Church to point out in what way the command could by all be literally fulfilled. Man is bidden to bring his offerings to God as an act of—

I. *Duty and Obedience.*—Simply because God wills that we should do so. How much thought, care, and vain speculation would be avoided if the commands of God were obeyed—1) Immediately, without any pause or hesitancy of mind; 2) Humbly, as feeling thoroughly confident that God knows far better than do we ourselves, what is best for us; 3) Cheerfully, feeling sure that God not only knows what is best for us, but ever acts towards us for the best. There can be no loss in keeping God's commandments.

II. *Discipline.*—There is a certain discipline involved in giving to God, for no God-fearing man would dare to offer to God that which cost him nothing; would dare, after making his own meal, to throw to

God the crumbs which had fallen from his table. Yet many so act; they grudge God anything which they themselves value. The command was given to teach man—1) The duty of self-sacrifice; 2) Of faith, or of trusting in God to repay that which is lent to Him; 3) Of obedience, as implying the submission of man's will to His own.

III. *Worship.*—An instinct not to come empty-handed into God's House or Presence; one acted upon by the Magi. Oblations or offerings were ever joined with prayers. While we ask of God, we are bound to lend our help towards carrying on His work in the world. Such offerings are a pledge of the sincerity of our worship, that it is not—1) mere lip-service; 2) formal; 3) careless; but worthy of some recompense, such joy and gladness does it bring to the soul.

IV. *Love.*—We love God, and therefore feel that we can never do enough for Him. Love prompts us to offer—1) Liberally, to the extent of our means; 2) gladly, with a glad heart; 3) prayerfully, that our gifts may be both blessed and accepted.

Epilogue.—" None shall appear before me empty." All have something to bring; for the empty-handed no excuse will be allowed at the last day.

SERMON XV.

THE CHRISTIAN'S SUNSET.

" Let not the sun go down upon your wrath."—*Eph.* iv. 26.

S. Augustine.—" This is to be received as spoken in a sacrament or mystery, for it is not to be understood of that sun which has a certain sublimity amongst the visible heavenly bodies; which can be seen alike both by ourselves and the beasts; but of that sun which the pure hearts of the faithful alone see, as it is said ' that was the true light, which lighteth every man that cometh into the world.' (S. John i. 9.) It is the light, truly, of justice and wisdom, which the mind ceases to see when by the perturbation of anger it shall have become as it were surmounted by a cloud, and then it is as if the sun set upon the wrath of man."—*Ser. de Diver.* xxii. vol. x. p. 433, D.

One object of our Blessed Lord's coming into the world, was to bring light and sunshine to men's hearts; that the nations which sat in darkness might

see the " great light " (S. Matt. iv. 16) of Him Who
said, " I am the light of the world." (S. John viii. 12;
ix. 5; xii. 46.) Hence the prophecy; " To those that
fear My Name shall the Sun of Righteousness arise
with healing in His wings." (Mal. vi. 2.) As the
natural sun—1) Warms the earth and fertilizes it, so
does the Spiritual Sun warm and fertilize the soul.
2) Makes all things bright with its own glory; so
does this other Sun glorify and brighten our common
life. 3) Drives away all the shades and powers of
darkness; so does " the Sun of Righteousness "
dispel doubt, sorrow, and fear, bringing gladness in its
train.

Jesus Christ shines upon the faithful as the sun—

I. *Lovingly.*—With no angered and darkened face
did Jesus Christ look down upon this world, but with
one full of sorrow and of love. Of sorrow for all that
man was called upon to suffer; of love, inasmuch as
man was very dear to Himself. They who now walk
worthily, look up with the eye of faith, and behold that
loving Sun still shining upon them. As such, it brings
to the mind—1) Peace; 2) Hope; 3) Glory;
gilding this common life with its bright rays. It
brings Jesus Christ home to the soul as our peace,
our hope, our glory, and exceeding great reward.

II. *Ever Shining.*—Unlike the natural sun which
departs leaving darkness in its train, this Sun never

sets. It maketh all our darkness to be light, and enlighteneth the very valley of the shadow of death. It never sinks below the horizon of the eye of faith, unless—1) Man turns away from it; 2) obscures it by the clouds of sin; 3) by desperation, plunges the soul in the depths of doubt.

III. *Healing.*—The natural sun sometimes—1) Scorches and burns up: the Spiritual Sun never puts forth moie heat than the weak soul can bear to endure; it warms, but does not dry up the heart. 2) Dazzles, by its excessive splendour. Jesus Christ shines only as men can bear His light. 3) Fatigues, shade is so welcome to the weary. This other Sun invigorates alone.

Epilogue.—Let not the True, Spiritual Sun go down upon your sin, your sorrow, and your doubt. Pray against a heart which is cold, dull, and dark. Part with all else, rather than with this sunshine of the soul. They are startling words to ring in man's ears, "If therefore the light that is in thee be darkness, how great is that darkness!" (S. Matt. vi. 23.)

SERMON XVI.

THE OLD MAN AND THE NEW.

" Put off concerning the former conversation, the old man . . . .
put on the new man."—*Ephes.* iv. 22-24.

S. Augustine.—"The temporal dispensation and
medicine of Divine Providence towards those who have
merited mortality by sin, is thus delivered. The
nature and bringing up of every man born is thus
designed. The first age, infancy, is to be entirely
forgotten by the growing one. Childhood follows this,
in which we begin to remember somewhat. To this
succeeds youth; after the labours of which, some peace
is granted to the more advanced age which, through
weakness and disease, leads to death. This is the
life of a living man who is bound up in the body and
with the desires of earthly things. He is called the
' old man,' and the ' outward man,' and the ' earthly
man;" although he may gain somewhat of that which
is commonly called happiness. Some from the
beginning of this life to its end, live only in it;

whilst others beginning necessarily from it are new-
born within, and spoil and slay these other parts, by
their spiritual strength, and by the increases of wisdom;
and they bind themselves by the heavenly laws until
death, after which, the whole will be renewed. This
one is called the ' new man,' the ' inward man,' and
the ' heavenly man,' having his certain distinct
spiritual ages, not according to the proportion of years,
but of advances. The first in the fruitful examples of
useful history. The second in the forgetfulness of
things human and the stretching forth to those which
are divine. The third, marrying and rejoicing the
more trusting and carnal appetite, by the power of
reason within, in a certain sweet wedlock; when soul
is joined to mind and overshadowed by the veil of
modesty, so that now it is not forced to live rightly,
but although all consent, it does not please to sin.
The fourth, more firmly and more ordered in the doing
and shining in perfect manhood; apt and fitted for
sustaining and dispersing all the persecutions, tem-
pests, and billows of this world. The fifth, at peace
and tranquil in every part, looking at the wealth and
abundance of the unchangeable Kingdom and of the
highest and ineffable wisdom. The sixth, of every

kind of change towards life eternal, even to the total forgetfulness of temporal life, passing over to the perfect form which is made after the image and similitude of God. The seventh is eternal rest and perpetual blessedness distinguished by no ages. For as the end of 'the old man' is death, so the end of 'the new man' is life eternal; the one is the man of sin, the other is the man of righteousness."—*De Verâ Relig.* cxxvi. vol. i. p. 275, H.

The advance in the Spiritual life, which is allegorically expressed by the putting off of the old man and the putting on of the new, implies four primary conditions.

I. *An Endeavour.*—The soul has long been sleeping in the lethargy of indifference and sin; it has failed to gain its due and proper powers from the quickening energy of love and grace. The old unregenerate life, nature, and desires, have been sufficient for it. An awakening is now taking place; the chrysalis is passing into the winged insect; to mount aloft on wings by which it can visit scenes of glory and of beauty. It feels now, for the first time, its own great —1) need; 2) imperfection; and 3) desire. A need of something that it has not, yet it ought to have; an imperfection, inasmuch as its powers are crippled and unable to supply its want; a desire to transgress the

F

old boundaries of its experience and its feelings, to reach forward towards those high and heavenly things which are before.

II. *A Union.*—In which the spirit and soul are united and made one with the Spirit of God. (1 Cor. vi. 17.) This union is—1) stronger than any mere earthly tie (Rom. viii. 35); 2) more enduring, it cannot be dissolved by death; 3) more ennobling, since it joins the soul to the Highest Goodness. Of such a soul, which has become the bride of Jesus Christ, it is true, that "old things are passed away."

III. *An Endurance.*—This indicates the spiritual manhood. A time of sore temptation, care, and trouble; a season in which must be borne the full heat and burden of the day. The strength given from above enables it, when temptation or sorrow come —1) to meet it boldly; 2) to sustain it nobly; 3) to conquer it entirely.

IV. *A rest and quietude.*—This is when the " new man " in the maturer age of its experience has become —1) conformed to God; 2) confident toward God; 3) joyful in God. (Rom. v. 2.)

Epilogue.—Seek to gain these successive growths in grace, by which the " new man " may be developed and strengthened until it attain to measure of the stature of the fulness of Jesus Christ.

SERMON XVII.

FEAR.

"I know not the man."—*S. Matt.* xxvi. 74.

S. Augustine.—"What dost thou, O Peter, what speakest thou? Thy voice is suddenly changed. Who is it that asketh thee, that thou hast so quickly answered? Not a slave; not a freedwoman; not a Pharisee; not a Scribe; not a priest; not a soldier; not a centurion; not an archer; not one who by his rule could inspire dread in one confessing. Not a woman only, but a girl, and not only a girl, but a door-keeper, doubtless a vile and abject dependant. O thing of wonder! A girl approaching dashed in pieces the faith of Peter, and pierced the wonderful solidity of Peter, not by a whirlwind, not by a shower, but by the smallest drop of dew. Peter could not endure the lip of a girl; when she spoke he was troubled. The discourse of the girl continued, and the immoveable column was shaken."—*De Temp. Ser.* cxxvi. vol. x. p. 278, B.C.

" What did the Lord ask Peter after IIis Resurrection, except ' Lovest thou Me' (S. John xxi. 15) ; and
it was not enough to ask this once, but it must be
asked again and again the third time. Fear thrice
denied ; love thrice confessed."—*In Joan. Tract v.
De Cap.* iii. vol. ix. p. 220, A.

" What great thing is it to fear punishment ? But
it is a great thing to love righteousness."—*De Ver.
Apost. Ser.* xviii. vol. x. p. 121, F.

" There is a servile fear, and there is a chaste fear ;
there is a fear lest thou shouldst suffer punishment ;
there is another fear lest thou shouldst lose righteousness. That fear lest thou shouldst suffer punishment
is servile. What great thing is it to fear punishment ?
This is common to the most wicked servant, and to
the most cruel thief. It is not a great matter to fear
punishment, but it is a great matter to love righteousness. Does he then who loves righteousness fear
nothing ? He fears indeed ; but not that he should fall
into punishment, but lest he should lose righteousness."
—*In Joan. Tract.* xliii., *De Cap.* viii. vol. ix. p. 113, C.

But for the infinite mercy of the Lord, this servile
fear of punishment would have utterly ruined S. Peter.
It made shipwreck of his former love, faith, confidence,

and service to the Lord. This craven dread of punishment or suffering, blotted out the records of a past life. A sad case of moral cowardice.

Like S. Peter, we too are often tempted by moral fear to deny that which we know to be true and right; to do or say that which we believe to be wrong. Fear renders us eminently untrue to ourselves. To—

I. *Our Grace.*—God gives a certain measure of grace to every baptized soul; a certain help from above; a certain light which is not of this world; a certain longing which nothing in this earth can satisfy. This grace must be carefully guarded, usefully used, and fruitfully manifested. " Quench not the Spirit." (1 Thess. v. 19.)

Now moral fear makes us distrust in our heavenly help. By it we are made to feel weak when we are indeed strong, and so we fall an easy prey to those circumstances, those evil habits which we are bound to resist. Fear makes us unwilling to trust ourselves to the heavenly light and guiding; it binds us down to walk by sight rather than by faith. Fear restrains our longings, breaks down our aspirations, places glory far away out of our sight. Oh, " receive not "— through fear—" the grace of God in vain," saying, " I know not the man " of divine grace.

II. *Our Powers.*—We often, through fear of failure ridicule, and present loss, give up a high pursuit, a course of noble action; the attempt to subdue some failing or some sin. Many more who are capable of great things, fail through fear of failure, rather than from presumption; fearing to undertake a matter beyond their powers, saying, "I know not the man" of the Will.

III. *Our Knowledge.*—How manifold are our sins against knowledge! How often does fear lead us to say and to do that we know to be wrong; to regard consequences more than principles. We know what is right, true, and Christlike; we consent through fear to what we also know is wrong, false, and devilish; saying, "I know not the man" of Knowledge.

IV. *Our Convictions.*—To do despite to knowledge is to sin against the understanding; to do despite to conviction is to sin against the heart; to outrage all our most cherished and hallowed associations and feelings; to reverse the course of the inner man. This process—1) Hardens. 2) Stays all progress. 3) Ends in bitter disappointment of spirit; saying, "I know not the man" of Conscience.

Epilogue.—Above all physical courage is moral courage; deeper, more subtle, more often tried; cherish it and nobly use it. "Be of good courage, and He shall strengthen your heart, all ye that hope in the Lord." (Ps. xxxi. 24.)

SERMON XVIII.

ETERNAL LIFE.

"This is life eternal, that they might know Thee the only true God, and Jesus Christ, Whom Thou hast sent."— *S. John* xvii. 3.

S. Augustine.—"Eternal life can never grow vile, and it ever grows sweet. If life be loved why is not true life sought? If life be loved, let such a life be sought as can never end. And if it is loved, why is it not sought? But if it be sought because it is not here, why do we not hasten to the place in which it is? How was it that Life itself willingly poured itself in upon us? For Christ is true God and eternal life. He came to us lost, and redeemed us found. True Life itself came to the region of mortal natures; it gave a taste of its flavour: we have tasted and seen how sweet it is. He went before us and invited us to follow; and shall we fear to follow to that so great gift of which we have received such a taste? Life came to thee, repay in turn and do you come to it.

He received the conveyance of death, that, passing over it, He might liberate thee; do thou also receive death, and when thou shalt have come to Him, thou shalt so be received by Him, that thou mayst never die."—*De Symb.* cxii. vol. ix. p. 273, C.

The Incarnation was a message of eternal life. The Son of God took upon Him the nature of man that He might minister eternal life to our race. This He does by way of—

I. *Taste.*—Eternal life is a state of perfect love, knowledge, and glory. Jesus Christ came on earth showing, teaching, and preaching, a new doctrine of love. It was by love that He drew men to Himself, and then led them onwards in His holy highway. He drew men " with the cords of a man and the bands of love." "I am the truth," "in Whom are hid all the treasures of wisdom and knowledge." One sweet of eternal life will be to know even as we are known. The Lord, as the Great Teacher, instructs men in the highest knowledge; by faith, by intuition, and by contemplation. Such instruction is an earnest of the fulness of knowledge which is reserved for the immortal state. Pray " that I may know Him."

II. *Invitation.*—Jesus Christ invites us to follow Him, Whom to know and follow is eternal life, which is a life of holiness, resignation, and worship. 1) By present subjugation of sin ; 2) by an entire resignation to the will of God; 3) by a devout and constant worship we are prepared to partake, with the holy, submissive, and worshipping spirits around the throne of God, of eternal life.

III. *Means.*—Jesus Christ is eternal since—1) He made death a passage to life (Heb. ii. 14), and became "the first-fruits of those who are sleeping." 2) He made an entrance to life, that whither the head had gone the members should follow; He took our nature within the veil. 3) He left with us the food of life, "the medicine of immortality." "Whoso eateth My Flesh and drinketh My Blood hath eternal life." (S. John vi. 54.)

Epilogue.—Seek to connect time with eternity; the life on earth with the life in heaven. Then will be the assurance ours. (Coloss. iii. 4.)

SERMON XIX.

THE BEAUTIFUL.

"Thine eyes shall see the King in His beauty."—*Isa.* xxxiii. 17.

S. Augustine.—"Although, O God, the soul is arrested amongst things beautiful, yet these have no existence apart from Thee."—*Confess.* iv. c. 10. vol. i. p. 37, H.

"What is a beautiful thing and what is beauty? What is it that attracts us and attaches us to the things which we love? Unless a grace and a beauty were in them by no means would they draw us to themselves."—*Confess.* iv. c. 13, vol. i. p. 38, F.

"The world itself, by its most orderly change and motion and by its appearance—the most beautiful of all visible things—although in some measure it is silent, yet it is able to proclaim itself to have been made—and this only save by a great God—made ineffably and invisibly, and by a beautiful God ineffably and invisibly."—*De Civit. Dei.* l. xi. c. 4. vol. v. p. 116, C.

" All beauty of body consists in the congruity of its parts with a certain suavity of colour."—*De Civit. Dei.* l. xxii. c. 19. vol. v. p. 282, A.

" What is righteousness when it is in us, or any other grace by which we live wisely and rightly, than the beauty of the inward man ? It is after this beauty rather than that of the body, that we have been made in the image of God."—*Epist. ad Consen.* vol. ii. p. 294, E.

" To us who believe the Bridegroom is beautiful wheresoever He may show Himself. Beautiful God, the Word with God ; beautiful in the womb of the Virgin, in which, not losing divinity, He assumed humanity. Beautiful, born the Infant Word, for whilst He was a suckling infant, carried by human hands, the heavens spoke ; the angels sang His praises ; the star led the Magi; He was adored in the manger. Beautiful, therefore, in heaven ; beautiful on earth ; beautiful in the womb; beautiful in the hands of His parents ; beautiful in His miracles ; beautiful in His stripes ; beautiful, inviting men to life ; beautiful, not taking care of death ; beautiful, laying down His soul ; beautiful, taking it back again ; beautiful on the Cross ; beautiful in the sepulchre ;

beautiful in heaven; beautiful in the understanding. Let not the infirmity of the flesh turn away your eyes from the splendour of His beauty. Righteousness is the true and the highest beauty."—*Enarr. in Psal.* xliv. vol. viii. p. 144, H.

Such is the promise to the holy, one day to behold God; not in His goodness only, or in His love, or in His power, or in His glory, but "in His beauty." God created us with a sense of beauty; He implanted in our souls a love of the beautiful; a love that should purify the heart and ennoble the life. He sent His Son on earth to realize the beautiful in Person, thought, and action. Amongst the various manifestations of the beautiful, we note—

I. *The Natural World.*—All the Universe is a thought of God, Who hath prepared for us, and placed us in, a world of exceeding beauty. Earth, air, sky, all teem with forms of beauty. The beautiful is over our heads and under our feet; on our right hand and on our left, wheresoever we may take our walks abroad. God's works in nature are full of beauty. Every flower and leaf and passing cloud should speak to us of God, and raise the soul to Him. In the natural world we note a beauty of—1) Design; it is a *kosmos.* 2) Form and colour. 3) Adaptation of means to end.

II. *The Artificial World.*—So called for distinction's sake; which distinction is essentially a false one, since man belongs to God, is His creature; and what man does, inasmuch as it is good and true, it is in a sense, done by God Himself. There is an elevating beauty in good and sublime pictures; in sculpture; in music; in high thoughts, whether written in prose or verse, whether read or spoken. Painter, sculptor, poet, writer, musician—all are fellow workers; all lift the soul above the daily life of toil, with its sin and sorrow; are all working together for the progress and development of our race. This beauty flows from—1) Harmony; 2) Proportion; 3) Realized conception.

III. *The Moral World.*—A beauty all its own, and very glorious in the earnest struggle which many make to overcome an untoward life; in the patient enduring of sorrow, suffering, and wrong; in the heroic self-sacrifice of which the common daily life of man affords so many examples. Beautiful, indeed, to see the old tended by the young; the sick, by the healthy; the parent, by the child; beautiful to find in a wan and suffering body, a spirit which no misfortune can subdue and pervert. This beauty is often—1) masked or hidden; 2) lowly in subject; 3) sublime in manifestation.

IV. *The Spiritual World.*—" The beauty of

holiness." Heaven will be a place of beauty and of beautiful worship. All the Apocalyptic glimpses of the heavenly worship are visions of the King in His beauty. So ought our earthly worship to be a copy of —The Beautiful in its—1) Earnestness; 2) Reverence; 3) Sumptuousness. The House of God ought to be grander than any house of man. There is a true beauty and glory in the worship of the Church on earth.

Epilogue.—All true beauty is summed up in the likeness to Him Who is absolutely beautiful. (See quotation from S. Augustine, in Psalm xliv., at page 75. " To us," etc.)

SERMON XX.

SMALL THINGS.

"Well done, thou good and faithful servant: thou hast been
faithful over a few things, I will make thee ruler over many
things: enter thou into the joy of thy lord."—*S. Matt.* xxv. 21.

S. Augustine.—"'Forgive us our debts, as we
forgive our debtors.' (S. Matt. vi. 12.) We do not
desire those things to be forgiven us which we do not
doubt were forgiven us at baptism, but those indeed,
which, although small, yet from the fragility of human
nature, creep upon us quickly. These, if gathered
together against us, will so weigh us down and oppress
us, as if they formed some one great sin. What
difference does it make to the sailor whether the ship
is buried and sunk by one large wave, or whether the
water creeping by little and little into the hold, and
being by negligence left alone and despised, fills and
sinks the ship?"—*Epist. ad Seleucianæ*, vol. ii.
p. 172, A.

Bearing in mind our Blessed Lord's great careful-

ness "to fulfil all righteousness," (S. Matt. iii. 15),
to comply with every precept of the moral law; the
small restriction which God placed upon Adam in
Paradise (Gen. ii. 17) as a test of obedience; how
David "poured" the water of Bethlehem "out unto
the Lord" (2 Sam. xxiii. 16); Naaman's disposition
to despise small things (2 Kings v. 11); we should be
most careful against offending God in little things;
we should carefully guard against sloth as to small
things. All things have small beginnings; fire, war,
holiness, sin, knowledge, etc. In God's sight the
distinction between things small and great does not
exist. Let us refer small things to Him, then we
shall learn their true value. Nothing is really small
which—

I. *Pleases or displeases God.*—Think upon God;
Who He is; what His mind is. Our finite minds are
lost in the contemplation of Him. That the mind of
God could be occupied with trifles, it were blasphemy
even to think. Whatsoever it may be, howsoever
small it may seem to be, it cannot be really small—1)
if it is worth God's thinking about; 2) if it is capable
of exciting in Him pleasure or anger; 3) if it brings
us near to, or keeps us far off, from Him. The idle
thought, or word, or deed is not rightly to be called
small or idle, when it can affect God and alter our
relationship to Him. The first and weakest aspira-

tion after holiness ; the first feeble temptation to sin ;
are both great events in His sight; yet they are
events at which the world would smile, if it should
condescend to notice them at all.

II. *Hinders or advances our perfection.*—If we had
a race to run which involved our future life in glory or
in shame, how careful we should be, lest undue
obstruction should be found in the road ; lest we
should be out of health ; lest our equipments should
not be in order. In clearing away obstacles to success
in life we scorn nothing, we deem nothing to be
beneath our notice. We seize every advantage ; are
verily "faithful over few things." Our progress and
our perfection, our success in this world, our salvation
in the next, depends upon—1) small beginnings ; 2)
small advances ; 3) small endeavours ever at work.
The greatest physical changes on the surface of the
globe, are the result of, comparatively speaking, small
forces exerting an unceasing action over indefinite
periods of years. In working out our salvation—1)
we should despise no helps ; 2) we should scorn to
notice no obstacles, however trifling they may seem
to be.

III. *Gains or loses a great reward.*—An event may
be small in itself, yet infinitely large in its consequences. The small sin ends in eternal loss ; the
small victory over temptation leads to an everlasting

G

reward.   Judge nothing to be small or great in itself,
but only so in relation to—1) Its aim or intention :
the cup of cold water, and the widow's mite.   2) Its
effect; how is it acting upon us? what is it doing for
us?   3) Its eternal consequence.

Epilogue.—Be thou "faithful over few things."
Cherish small opportunities, means, knowledge, goodness, beginnings, and hereafter greater and the greatest
things will be thine.   With wonder and gratitude you
will look back upon the past; your grateful expression
will be, "By the grace of God I am what I am."

SERMON XXI.

MAN'S THREE ESTATES.

"Thou hast made him a little lower than the angels."—*Ps*. viii. 5.

S. Augustine.—"There is a nature which is change-able in relation to place and time; as is the body. There is a nature which is changeable in relation to time, but not to place, as is the soul. Lastly, there is a nature which cannot be changed either by time or place; this is God. You see verily, in this distribu-tion of nature, that which occupies the highest place; that which occupies the lowest place, and yet exists; that which occupies a middle place, being above the lowest and beneath the highest.

"The highest is itself blessedness; the depth, that which can be neither blessed nor miserable. The middle lives miserably when it inclines to the lowest; whilst by turning to the highest it lives happily.

"He who believes in Christ, does not love the lowest, does not boast of the middle, and so becomes fit to

G 2

cling to the highest; and this is the sum of that which we are commanded, advised, and excited to do."—*Epist. ad Cœles.* vol. ii. p. 107, D.

Yes! man is created a "little lower than the angels," inasmuch as he has a perishable material body: yet is he capable of becoming "equal to the angels," inasmuch as he is made in the image and likeness of God. Man partakes of three estates or natures.

I. *The lowest.*—We are in this present life surrounded by the third and lowest nature or estate. There is on every side to be encountered the estate of 1) Sin, which is an estate of loss. Sin is not only a breaking of the laws of God, but an infinite loss to man. God's laws, whether moral, physical, or revealed, are calculated to develope man to the greatest possible extent—they are not merely prohibitive—" trespassers will be prosecuted," but they are educational and disciplinal. The more we can obey, the more perfect will become our nature and our life; for "His commandments are not grievous." 2) Of Sloth; which takes various forms. Sloth in feeling, in realizing our position, in bringing home to the soul the infinite lovingkindness and mercy of God. Sloth in the failing to turn all God's gifts to the best and holiest account. Sloth in letting the circumstances of life drift us whither they please, unmindful of our own powers and free will. 3) Sorrow, which acts like mud to the feet, and lead to the wings, holding down the soul from any high ascent into the region of faith and love.

II. *The highest.*—This is Godlike ; not in relation to the future heaven of glory only, but also in relation to all that is good, true, and beautiful here on earth. It consists, 1) In trueness to our higher nature ; in cultivating all that is a gain ; in ever reaching onwards and upwards towards perfection. 2) In acting in all things as if guided by a faith, which leads us from the present imperfection to a future of perfect justice, re-tribution, and reward.

III. *The middle.*—Our present state and nature, lower yet higher than the angels. This is a state of : 1) Discipline and trial ; 2) Preparation for higher and better things hereafter ; 3) Doubt and uncertainty. Even such was Adam's state in Paradise. Hence we learn never to say " It is enough !" and so to leave off further effort.

Epilogue.—Shall this middle state lead upwards or downwards ? joining you to all that is great and good, or for ever degrading you, your birthright being lost ?

SERMON XXII.

THE POWER OF THE FUTURE.

" Have tasted the powers of the world to come."—*Heb.* vi. 5.

S. Augustine.—" Thou, therefore, the Governor of Thy creature; how dost Thou teach minds concerning future things ? Thou hast taught Thy prophets. What is the manner by which Thou teachest things future to him for whom there is no future ; or, rather, by the present, the things which are to come. It has forced itself upon me, that of myself I am not able to learn of myself; but I am able to learn by Thee when Thou sweetly shalt have given light to my darkened eyesight." —*Confess.*, xi. c. 19, vol. i. p. 75, D.

Many live without ever having " tasted the powers of the world to come," or felt the influences of their eternal future. Many live, either as if they were immortal in the body, or were mortal in the soul : as if they were either to live in this world for ever, or else to cease to be, when this life shall end.

There are " powers of the world to come," which

must be felt or tasted now. There are shadows of the future which either darken or enlighten the present. By experience, energy, sorrow, suffering, and prosperity, we "taste the powers" of this present world, living in its influences, sympathising with its every impulse. By carrying onwards and upwards this experience and energy, we taste "the powers of the world to come"; we feel the influences of the future; and the holier and the higher is our life, the more do we experience their effects upon us. We, if we ever reflect as Christians at all, taste "the powers of the world to come" in our sense of a coming future which awakens:

I. *Fear and dread.*—A reflective mind cannot wholly put its conscience to sleep. It may sleep long and undisturbedly, but after a sudden fall into sin, or at the hour of death, there comes a terrible and retributive awakening.

It is the "power of the world to come," forcing itself home to the sinful heart; bringing remorse for lost opportunity, a sense of bitter shame and humiliation in its being so untrue to itself, and to that which it ought to be. A fear and dread of the great unknown, carrying in its background an account to be taken of this present life.

II. *Holiness.*—The desire, in part at least, to be prepared for so great a change. Holiness consists in 1) A freedom and purification from sin; 2) a putting on of the garments meet for heaven ;　3) in the likeness to Jesus Christ Himself.　I taste "the powers of the world to come," and I desire that pardon for sin, by which alone I can obtain an entrance into heaven ; that clothing which shall not make me ashamed in the presence of saints and angels; that mark or likeness to the Lord which is the sealing of God's elect.

III. *Patience.*—The more I taste " the powers of the world to come," the shorter and less important seems to be this present life: "a little while," indeed, as compared with that eternal future, the power of which is upon me now.

IV. *Hope.*—There are such things as promises in Revelation, promises of happiness, glory, honour, and immortality and eternal life in the kingdom of God. Promises to make the heart leap up with joy and thankfulness, to enkindle in holy souls a desire to depart and to be with Jesus Christ.　These promises are " powers of the world to come."

Epilogue.—To " have tasted the powers of the world to come " is—1) to be prepared for that coming world ;　2) to be supported and purified in this our present state of sorrow and of probation.　Oh ! wretched improvidence, to taste only that which is so fleeting and so false, and not to taste the powers which are eternal.

SERMON XXIII.

EQUAL UNTO THE ANGELS.

"Equal unto the Angels."—*S. Luke* xx. 36.

S. Augustine.—" A certain magnificence is in the Angels, and so great power, that, if they did all things which they were able to do, it could not be endured. Every man desires the power of the Angels, but their righteousness he does not love. First love righteousness, and power will follow you."—*Enarr, in Psal.* xcv. vol. viii. p. 386, G.

In many other things, besides power, we covet the attributes of the Angels. We think with longing, lingering thoughts, and we gaze with sad and wistful eyes, upon their happiness, their immortality, their glory, their nearness and likeness to God ; and then we turn away, as from a vision of brightness in which we have neither lot nor part; we turn away, with a saddened and more hopeless feeling than we had before; a new light was given unto us for a little season, and soon it was all again turned to darkness and to sorrow.

These words "Equal unto the Angels" suggest a threefold vision.

I. *A Vision afar off.*—The beginning of the spiritual life is like the beginning of day. There is a time of darkness; the heart is heavy with the sleep of sin, and the eyes of the soul are surrounded by the blackness of the night of ignorance and folly. The dawn comes at last; an enlightening, hardly perceptible, yet steadily advancing; a streak of light breaking the dull monotony of the horizon; a bright but weak and distant sun at length appears. What is all the awakening of nature, but a type of man's soul awakening from the death of sin unto the life of righteousness; from the lowly life of this suffering nature, to the spiritual life which is "equal unto the Angels?" Firstly, a sense of darkness and weariness oppresses the soul; then follow the signs and tokens, few and slight, of a coming deliverance. Afterwards does the heaven above the soul indeed seem to open and a voice is heard bidding the conscience "come and see." Still, without the soul, are all God's promises of grace and mercy; they are but as the sounds of a pleasant voice.

II. *The Vision drawing near.*—The sun has risen: all things are enlightened by his beams. It is a time to gaze, to analyse, and to learn. "Equal unto the Angels." What is an Angel and an Angel's life?

We must seek the Kingdom of God by—1) Meditation ; 2) prayer ; 3) instruction. The things without us must be made our own. Spiritual food must be assimilated so as to form a part of our spiritual life.

III. *The Vision realized.*—The promise is made to the holy dead, "Neither can they die any more, for they are equal unto the Angels" (S. Luke xx. 36) ; but in this life the promise is in part fulfilled, the vision is in part realized. 1) Do I want power ? "I can do all things." (Philipp. iv. 13.) "My grace is sufficient." (2 Cor. xii. 9.) 2) Do I long for immortality ? "He that believeth on Me hath everlasting life. (S. John vi. 47.) 3) Am I seeking for happiness ? "The Kingdom of God is joy." (Rom. xiv. 17.) 4) Is glory my desire ? "I will glory of the things which concern mine infirmities." (2 Cor. xi. 30.) 5) Is nearness to God my aim ? "The pure in heart shall see God." (S. Matt. v. 8.)

Epilogue.—The angelic life of heaven is to begin in part on earth, by partaking of the elements of holiness and knowledge.

SERMON XXIV.

THE FOURFOLD SENSE OF HOLY SCRIPTURE.

"Search the Scriptures."—*S. John* v. 39.

S. Augustine.—" All Scripture which is called the Old Testament is narrated in a fourfold sense to those who desire to study it diligently; according to the history, the ætiology, the analogy, and the allegory. It is narrated according to the history, when that which is written or hath been done is taught; according to the ætiology, when the cause is shown for which anything is either done or said; according to the analogy, when the two Testaments are demonstrated to harmonize; according to the allegory, when it is taught that what is written is not to be taken in a literal sense, but is to be figuratively understood. Our Lord Jesus Christ and His Apostles used all these methods of interpretation. The objection to the Disciples plucking the ears of corn was met by an appeal to history. (S. Matt. xii. 3; 1 Sam. xxi. 4.)

The Lord's argument against divorce belongs to the ætiological sense. (S. Matt. xix. 9.) Moses permitted it beneficially for a time, and this which Christ was commanding seems to point to other seasons. Concerning the analogy, by which is perceived the agreement of both Testaments, it is sufficiently to be found, as I think, in the New Testament. It remains to treat of allegory. Our Liberator Himself used in the Gospel an allegory taken from the Old Testament. (S. Matt. xii. 39.) What, too, shall I say of Paul? He treated the history in Exodus as an allegory of the future Christian people. (1 Cor. x. 1-12.) Also again Paul said to the Galatians, (Gal. iv. 22-31; Gen. xvi. 15; xxi. 2)."—*De Utilitate Credendi*, c. iii. vol. vi. p. 32, H.

According to the old distich the senses of Holy Scripture were somewhat differently arranged :—

" Litera gesta docet ; quid credas allegoria ;
Moralis quid agas ; quo tendis anagogia."

The value of having four interpretations of Holy Scripture is very great. 1) It gives us four Bibles instead of one. We see the mind of God under four different aspects. 2) It gives us a new interest in Holy Scripture, there is something for us to discover for ourselves; to work out and to apply. Taking the senses in order we note—

I. *The Historical Sense.*—There is much beauty and instruction in " the letter " only of Holy Scripture. Its histories are so—1) Truthful; they carry the conviction of the mind with them, when they are read. 2) Simple; no guile or double purpose in them; a simple record of the workings of God's providence at various times of the world's history. 3) Affecting; the Bible histories are full of feeling, *e.g.*, the death of Rachel; the recognition of Joseph's brethren; the parting between David and Jonathan; the raising of Lazarus. Hence these narratives refresh us, soothing a troubled soul, and bringing the Fatherhood of God very nigh unto us.

II. *The Ætiological or Moral Sense.*—This gives the application of that which is recorded as happening so many centuries ago. It in part reveals—1) the purpose which God had in view in so ordering things. 2) The lessons which we are to learn from these events. " They are written for our admonition." (1 Cor. x. 11.) Hence this moral sense does not leave a history merely as a history, but as a record which speaks to ourselves in tones either of love or warning, of either admonition or encouragement.

III. *The Allegorical Sense.*—This sense reveals that which is signified under the garb of imagery.

The Lord's Parables are allegories, and some of these He has Himself explained. Nearly all the chief personages of the Old Testament history are allegorical, and all the events have a spiritual meaning which is deeper, and more evangelical, than the moral reading. This spiritual or allegorical sense looks " within the veil." 1) It refers all things to the kingdom of grace ; like the sacrifices which pointed to the one sacrifice on Calvary. 2) It interprets the things which are seen in reference to the things which are out of sight ; and so it invests the smallest and commonest events with a new and lasting glory and dignity.

IV. *The Anagogical or Analogical Sense.*—This leads time up to eternity ; earth to heaven ; the Church Militant to the Church Triumphant ; the kingdom of grace to the kingdom of glory. The Law is absorbed into the Gospel, and the Gospel into the Beatific Vision. Hence all Scripture becomes one great and glowing prophecy of glory.

Epilogue.—" Search the Scriptures " with faith, prayer, and the desire to learn and to obey ; so will you ascend from sense to sense, and from one glory of the Bible to another ; being led by the Spirit of truth into all truth.

SERMON XXV.

THE VALUERS OF THE SOUL.

"What shall a man give in exchange for his soul?"—*S. Matt.* xvi. 26.

S. Augustine.—" The nature of the soul is more excellent than the nature of the body, it excels greatly; it is a thing spiritual, incorporeal, akin to the substance of God. It is a something invisible; it governs the body; it moves the members of it; it directs the senses: it prepares the thoughts; it exerts the actions; it receives the images of things which are infinite. And in short, dearly beloved, who is sufficient for the praises of the soul."—*Enarr. In Psalmum* cxlv. vol. viii. p. 604. E.

Such are some of the offices of the soul; of that immortal nature by the possession of which we are related to God. What value do we set upon it? What are we giving in exchange for its eternity of happiness, perfection, and glory? The text speaks of only one; but there are three valuers of the soul; three, who make an exchange for it.

I. *The Lord Jesus Christ.*—He values the soul at so high a price, that, in exchange for it, He, of His own free will, gave up—1) His life of glory in heaven, coming upon this earth in our lowly nature ; 2) His full and perfect happiness, to carry the burden of sin— His spiritual Cross—all the ingratitude, contradiction, and agony of His suffering life as "a man of sorrows;" 3) His human life, for the life of the souls of men. "The redemption of their souls is precious." (Ps. xlix. 8.)   So now, for the refreshing of the soul, He gives Himself.

Besides all this, note how careful He ever was that the soul should not be "offended" or "scandalized;" how loving, yet how strict, a Guardian He was of the souls of the young.   No one ever valued the soul as highly as did Jesus Christ ; no one ever sacrificed themselves for it as He did, because He also was God and man.   He alone knows the high value that God sets upon the soul : He alone knows the workings and experiences of a life in heaven and a life in hell. We should tremble, noting the great price at which the Lord valued the soul.   What did Jesus Christ give in exchange for the soul ?   All that as God and man He held most dear ; Himself, body, soul, and spirit.

II. *Satan.*—He values the human soul very highly; hence he spares no pains to make it his own.   Satan

1) never tires, he is always attacking the holy soul,
and leading the wicked onwards into greater sin.   He
tempted David to number the people (1 Chron. xxi. 1);
Job to curse God (Job i. 12); Judas to betray his Lord
(S. Luke xxii. 3); he sifted S. Peter.   (id. 31.)   2)
Uses every device; as at the Temptation of our Lord.
3) Strains every point to pervert all things, and to
change every blessing into a curse.   Satan gives much
in exchange for a soul—energy, thought, and much
care.

III. *Man himself.*—What shall a man give in exchange for his soul?   Others value it at a high price;
what value do you set upon it?   1) What care do you
take of it?   How do you discipline, instruct, and
clothe it?   2) What sacrifices are you making for it?
Is it your child, the Lord's darling? (Ps. xxxv. 17.)
What are you denying yourself for its sake?   Will
you give up a right hand or a right eye for it?   Are
you willing to preserve it at any cost?   3) Is it
more to you than all else?   Is its salvation your
chiefest and highest concern?

Epilogue.—Shame, oh, shame! if we will barter for
a worthless bauble that which both Jesus Christ and
Satan so highly prize.

SERMON XXVI.

THE JOY OF HOLINESS.

"They that were foolish took their lamps, and took no oil with them."—*S. Matt.* xxv. 3.

S. Augustine.—"For although many hope great things from the goodness of Christ, yet have they no joy, so long as they do not live continently, save in the praises of men. They have therefore 'no oil with them.' For I judge that joy itself is signified by oil, since it is said, 'God, thy God, hath anointed thee with the oil of gladness.' (Ps. xlv. 7.) He does not rejoice who does not please God within. 'But the wise took oil in their vessels with their lamps;' that is, they placed in the heart and conscience the joy of good works, as the Apostle advises: 'Let every man prove his own work, and then shall he have rejoicing in himself and not in another.'"—*Lib. Octogint. Quæst.* 2. lii. vol. iv. p. 215. E.

There is, therefore, in this life a certain joy in holiness, just as there is a sorrow and fear in sin. The

paths of religion are verily paths of peace. Of this
joy of holiness we note that it is—

I. *Deep.*—It reaches to the recesses of the inner-
most soul. There is much joy in the world which
leaves a certain portion of the heart untouched. Such
joy is not superficial merely; the affections of home
and of life are not superficial; but they reach only to
a certain depth; there is a zone like that in a deep
sea-sounding which they touch not. A sense of
pardoned sin, of the abiding love of Jesus Christ, is
the very fount of our being "a well of [living] water,
springing up into everlasting life." This joy is deep;
for—1) Sorrow cannot reach it; 2) Sin cannot ex-
tinguish it, since, possessing it, sin can only be of
infirmity, and not of habit and will; 3) Disappointment cannot quench it.

III. *Lasting.*—The life of holiness brings a lasting
joy, which survives every storm, and outlives the tempest of passion and of pain. It does not depend upon—
1) that which is temporary; 2) that which can perish;
3) upon life itself. A priceless possession to carry this
joy in the soul for ever.

III. *Satisfying.*—All earthly joy is like the rose
with its thorn: it leaves a void, it is only in part complete; if it for a time satisfies the affections, it dis-
appoints the will, or the memory, or the understanding.
The joy of holiness ministers to every faculty. It is a

token that—1) the affections are set upon God ; 2) the will is in obedience ; 3) the memory is in a state of gratitude for past mercies ; 4) the understanding is in subjection to faith.

IV. *Ennobling.*—1) It lifts up the soul in exultation to God, and to all that is good and great ; 2) it casts every craven doubt and fear out of the heart ; and 3) it gives, as it were, angels' wings, upon which we are borne up over all the vicissitudes of time and life.

Epilogue.—With this joy at heart, we are ever ready to meet the Bridegroom, whether He comes to us in— 1) Sorrow ; 2) temptation ; 3) visitation : summoning us by the Angel of Death.

SERMON XXVII.

UNHOLY SELF-LOVE.

"Perilous times shall come, for men shall be lovers of their own selves."—2 *Tim.* iii. 1, 2.

S. Augustine.—" Self-love was the first ruin of man ; for if man had not loved himself, he would have put God before himself ; he would have desired ever to be in subjection to God. Not being in such subjection, he turned away from the will of God to do his own will. To love self is to desire to do one's own will. Learn to love thyself by not loving thyself. That you may know it to be a sin to love thyself, the Apostle says, ' For men shall be lovers of themselves.' And does not he who loves himself trust in himself ? Having forsaken God, a man begins to love himself ; but he is soon allured away from himself to love those things which are without himself. Hence the Apostle continues, ' covetous ' or lovers of money. You see that already you ' are without.' You began to love yourself ; remain in yourself, if you can. Art thou a

lover of money, by which thou art enriched ? Thou
hast begun to love that which is without thee, thou
hast betrayed thyself. When the love of a man goes
onwards from himself to those things that are without,
he begins to be consumed by that which is vain, and
like the Prodigal to waste his powers ; he is wasted
away ; he is emptied ; he is rendered destitute ; he feeds
swine, and labouring in the tending of cattle, at last he
recollects, and says, ' How many hired servants,' etc.
(S. Luke xv. 17.) When does he say this ? ' When
he comes to himself.' To come to himself, he must
have gone out of himself. Inasmuch as he had fallen
from himself he had gone out of himself; he first
returns to himself, that he may return to him whence
he had gone out of himself. ' He came to himself '
not to remain in himself, for he said, ' I will arise, and
go to my father.' Behold ! by what means he had
fallen from himself ; he had fallen from his father !
he had fallen from himself to those things which are
without ; he had gone out of himself. He returns to
himself, and goes to his father, where he could most
safely preserve himself. By returning to himself that
he may go to his father, he denies himself. What is
it to deny self ? Not to presume upon self ; to feel

oneself to be man ; to regard the prophetic saying,
' Cursed be the man that trusteth in man' (Jer. xvii. 5) ;
to lead oneself away from self that so one may cleave
to God ; to attribute to God all that is good, to self
all that is evil ; He says to such an one, ' Let him
deny himself.' "—*De Diversis. Ser.* xlvii. c. 2. vol. x.
p. 468, A.

A certain self-love is an instinct which was im-
pressed by God Himself upon our moral nature. "No
man hateth his own flesh." (Eph. v. 29.) Self-love
and self-preservation are parts of the same great law
of our being. There can be no proper self-respect
without a certain self-love, without which there can be
exercised no moral influence. We are all lovers of
self, and we were intended by God to be so. Why,
then, is self-love put by the Apostle in such ugly
company ? Why is it held up as a sign of perilous
times. It is insubordinate, unholy, and undue self-
ove which is here condemned ; a self-love which leads
to three great spiritual falls.

I. *Away from God.*—It is a universal law that
God is to be loved before all else ; and His Will obeyed
before all else. Self-love places—1) The will of man
in opposition to the will of God, as in the cases of
Adam, Saul, Pharaoh, etc. 2) The affections upon

the creature rather than upon the Creator; Samson
and Delilah. 3) The reason of our limited understanding against a holy faith in the revelation of
God.

II. *Away from man's true self.*—The soul cannot
rest in itself. When it leaves God it goes out of
itself into external things. The soul or self is—1)
The abode of an undying, accusing conscience.
2) Unsatisfied by itself; it cannot fulfil its own
wants. 3) It is incomplete, unless it be joined with
something else. It demands either some one to serve,
or some strong heart upon which to lean.

III. *Away from that which is really good.*—Self-
love leads the soul away from that which is good, from
God; from its true self to that which is—1) Deceitful;
2) unprofitable; 3) sinful. Case of the Prodigal
Son.

Epilogue.—Aim at (1 Cor. vi. 17) then love of self
becomes the love of God.

SERMON XXVIII.

HOLY SELF-LOVE.

" Thou shalt love the Lord thy God with all thy heart, and with all thy soul, and with all thy strength ; and thy neighbour as thyself."—*S. Luke* x. 27.

S. Augustine.—"Love the Lord, and so learn to love yourselves ; that when by loving the Lord ye shall have loved yourselves, ye may securely love your neighbour as yourselves. And who is there, you will say, who does not love himself? Who is there? See 'He that loveth iniquity hateth his own soul.' (Ps. xi. 5.) Does he love himself who loves his body, and hates his soul to his own hurt, to the hurt both of his body and soul? And who loves his own soul? He that loveth God with all his heart and with all his mind. To such an one I would at once entrust his neighbour."—*Ser.* vol. x. p. 712, B.

The Love of God shed abroad in the heart teaches a man that holy, true self-love which he must possess if he would rightly love his neighbour. This holy, pure self-love is divine in origin ; blessed in being ;

gracious in its effects and operations; it flows from the love of God; it sanctifies all life and being, and it spreads itself graciously over other hearts. Such blessed and blessing self-love which enables its possessor to fulfil the two great commandments of the law, is—

I. *Whole.*—It extends to the whole nature of man, body, soul, and spirit, leaving no part of man unconsecrated by its influence. Some—1) Love their bodies at the expense of their souls; sensually fulfilling all its animal desires and passions, and bringing the soul into a slavish captivity which is worse than death. 2) Love their souls or understandings at the expense of the body, injuring it by neglect and by a wanton disregard to its requirements and laws. 3) Have small love or care either for body or soul, leaving both ill-cared for; the mind ill-graced, ill-educated; the body unkempt and unattractive. When we love God altogether in His glory and majesty as far as we can know Him, and when we long to become like Him, then no part of His image and likeness will we willingly suffer to be defiled.

II. *Eternal.*—As God loved us with an everlasting love, so with a like love ought we to love ourselves. The love of Jesus is not limited to or hindered by death; nay, He loved Lazarus dead more almost than when he was living. True self-love, founded upon the love of God, must be eternal. Some love themselves for this transitory world only, fixing all their thought, care, and affection upon things of time, sense, and knowledge as related to this present life, without any love for, or care of themselves as they shall be for ever and ever when this world shall have passed away from them. Eternal self-love is—1) Wise : it excludes a passing present ; it includes an everlasting future. 2) Unlimited : has no short period in which to exercise itself. 3) Satisfying the soul, since it ranges beyond time.

III. *Profitable.*—God's love to us is full of profit and gain to us, and our love to Him brings blessings innumerable in its train. So must that true self-love be profitable, inasmuch as it is the product of our love of God. It embraces the love of that which concerns —1) Our eternal state ; our love of heaven and of that holiness which is the shadow of the life of heaven here below. 2) Our highest concerns; the purification of conscience and the development of the kingdom of grace within us. 3) Our best and most consistent course of life; leading to success and blessings in this life, and greater blessings in the life to come. If we truly value heaven ourselves, and the soul's highest interests, and a noble course of life, we cannot but seek to make others participants in these blessings.

IV. *Devoted.*—God's love to us is so devoted, that all our transgression and ingratitude cannot turn it away from us. "He loves unto the end" of our day of probation, even if we should die in sin and forfeit His love for evermore. Godlike self-love is devoted too. It is—1) Faithful; ever reminding us of duty and the goal before us. 2) Constant; never forsaking us when we are most untrue to ourselves, but cheering us with bright hopes of pardon and grace in our darkest hours. 3) Unselfish; hindered not by ingratitude.

Epilogue.—"As thyself," with this whole, eternal, profitable, and devoted self-love is thy neighbour to be loved; watered by the overflowings of thine own cup of love and of kindness. A man who loves God, and himself as loving Him, and his neighbour "as" himself, is one whose present life is happy, sustained, and blessed; whose death must be peaceful; whose eternity will be gloriously passed in the Presence of that God Who "is love."

SERMON XXIX.

THE MEEK.

"Blessed are the meek: for they shall inherit the earth."
—*S. Matt.* v. 5.

S. Augustine.—" I believe this earth to be that of which the Psalmist speaks : ' Thou art my portion in the land of the living.' (Ps. cxlii. 5.) This land signifies a certain solidity and stability of perpetual inheritance, in which the soul by a good affection rests as if in its own place ; just as the body does on earth ; and it is nourished by its own food, as the body is nourished by the ground. This is the rest and the life of the holy."—*De Serm. Dom. in Mont.* c. ii. vol. iv. p. 292, H.

The meek, in the journey of life, are like the weak and feeble in a crowded thoroughfare—they are sent to the wall, whilst others pass on before them. The promise does not hold good to this present earth which is so soon to be parted with ; but it does hold good for that spiritual and eternal land, " the land of the living ;" that is the land of deathless and holy souls. The meek have a life and an " earth " of their own, in which they find—

I. *Rest.*—The wind and tempest ruffles the surface of the ocean, but only to a certain depth. In the roughest sea it is calm after a few fathoms have been gained. The winds of this world's—1) Hate, stirs not up the soul of the meek, for it penetrates but a little way into the meek soul; it is deprived of any great power to wound; it is taken as a portion of the needful discipline of life. 2) Sorrow leaves the meek soul likewise calm, for it has deeply learned the lesson of resignation; it sees God's Fatherly, yet chastening, hand in every misfortune and sorrow that here afflicts the soul. 3) Opposition: for the meek and gentle soul holds on to its own as the reed bending to the storm retains its hold on the soil, whilst the sturdy oak is shattered and destroyed. The life of Jesus Christ—one of bitter experience, sorrow for other's sins, of opposition from those whom in love He came to save; yet He said, "Learn of Me, I am meek and lowly in heart, and ye shall find rest unto your souls." (S. Matt. xi. 29.)

II. *Food.*—Reflection is the true food of the soul; and the meek are nourished by this food, since there is no ground for remorse in the reflection upon—1) Forgiven injuries; which lose all their sting when they are forgiven, and form a nourishment instead of a root of bitterness for the soul. 2) Patient endurance; by which seeming curses are changed to blessings.

III. *Shelter.*—The soul of the meek finds its shelter in holy hope; for the meek both know and feel that they are the recipients of this beatitude. The hope full of immortality is theirs; as learners in the school of Jesus Christ they confidently look onwards and forwards to their school-house being one day changed into the mansions of the Father's house.

Epilogue.—Meek and holy souls have one "earth" of their own even here, still looking forward to a more glorious "earth" beyond the grave.

SERMON XXX.

THE HOUSE OF LAZARUS.

"Martha received Him into her house. And she had a sister called Mary."—*S. Luke* x: 38-39.

"An unholy life, truly, was far from that house; it was neither with Martha, nor with Mary. Two lives therefore remained in that house which had received the Lord, in the two women; both innocent, both laudable; one laborious, the other unemployed; neither wicked, neither slothful. There were in that house these two lives, and Himself the fountain of life. In Martha was an image of things present, in Mary of things to come. What Martha was doing, we are doing now; what Mary was doing this we hope to do. Let us do the former well that we may have the latter fully."—*De Verb. Dom.* xxvii. vol. x. p. 39, B.C.

This house of Lazarus is a type of the regenerate soul in which there dwells—

I. *Jesus—the "fountain of life," in thought.*—The Presence of Jesus in the house of the soul is a spiritual

I

presence, even as the soul itself is a spiritual existence; not subject to any of those material considerations which affect the body. A "fountain of life" to it inasmuch as Jesus Christ dwelling in the soul—1) Refreshes it. As in the desert, barren of life and vegetation, parched and dry, an oasis is formed around the fountain; the palm and other trees and shrubs bearing witness to its refreshing powers; so in the moral desert, or the care-worn, world-scorched soul, Jesus is a refreshing stream which renovates after fatigue, and lightens sorrow. 2) Supplies it. The fountain supplies the wants of all who enjoy its use. This spiritual fountain supplies wisdom, strength, holiness, and the other Christian graces. "My God shall supply all your need." 3) Never fails it. A true fountain never fails in the season even of the greatest drought. Our spiritual fountain is never dry, never exhausted; nay, the more we draw from it the larger becomes its supply. The well-spring of grace in Jesus Christ is infinite; and being unlimited, it never at any time can cease to flow. 4) Beautifies it. There is always beauty around a fountain; beauty of sight, from the sweet forms of vegetable life which flourish in its neighbourhood; of sound, from the babbling flow of its prattling waters. So Jesus glorifies and beautifies the soul in which He dwells; causing therein the growth of whatsoever things are lovely and of good report. Jesus is a fountain of light to the understanding ; of strength to the will ; of joy to the memory.

II. *Martha—life in action.*—" An image of things present" from whom we learn that our work in this world and life ought to be—1) Diligent. "Diligent in business." Diligence supplies many a defect; it makes up for the loss of many a happy opportunity; it always brings a blessing with it; not only in its results, but in its indirect action, upon the diligent themselves. 2) Earnest; both on account of the shortness of life, and of the amount of work which God has given each one of us to do in this short life; and the bearing which this present life has on the life to come. "Let us do the former well, that we may have the latter fully." 3) Persevering; never giving up or giving way. This life is our season of toil and care ; is the dispensation of our "Martha life," and in due time we shall reap if we faint not.

III. *Mary—life in rest.*—"An image of things to come," when this "Fountain of Life" Himself will be all in all. This life implies—1) A drawing near to Jesus, by knowledge and by love, and so being brought into the sphere of grace and light. 2) A sitting in quiet near Him, with a soul hushed from all the tumults of the world and of the flesh. 3) At His very feet : which betokens humility, as choosing the lowest place ;

reverence : acknowledging His majesty ; subjection : as offering to obey Him ; imitation : as truly resolving to follow His steps.   4) To hasten to catch the faintest breathings of His divine word and spirit, that so the soul may purely and truly receive the doctrine which the Master teaches.

Epilogue.—These three persons, assembled in the house of Lazarus, are from each other dissimilar ; representative, and yet harmonious ; and they signify unto us the continuity of life ; the dependence of the future upon the present.   They teach us that grace and holiness are to be cherished ; that every power is to be employed to the uttermost, if from the toil of this lower world we hope to ascend and to gain that rest which remaineth for the people of God.

SERMON XXXI.

THE DAY OF LIFE.

"Evening, and morning, and at noon, will I pray and cry aloud."
—*Ps.* lv. 17.

S. Augustine—"Evangelize thou and be not silent; declare that which thou hast received. In the 'evening,' of that which is past; in the 'morning' of that which is to come; 'at noon' of things sempiternal. The Lord in the 'evening' was on the Cross; in the 'morning' in the Resurrection; 'at noon' in the Ascension. And I will narrate in the 'evening' the patience of Him dying; I will announce in the 'morning' the life of resurrection; I will pray 'at noon' that He, 'sitting at the right hand of the Father' may hear me."—*Enarr. in Psal.* lv. vol. viii. p. 192, H.

The natural day is a true type of the day of life; and the Lord of Life during His earthly course, conformed to this type, and for all time hallowed it to the faithful. The periods of the day correspond with the periods of life ; and each reads a lesson to the thoughtful Christian mind.   In both days we note alike—

I. *An Evening.*—This time speaks to us " of that which is past."   The day has gone for weal or woe, for joy or sorrow it has departed.   Its hours, hopes, fears, opportunities, never can come back again. Every evening is a silent, though eloquent, preacher of the last evening, to be followed in this world by that night in which no man can work.   In the evening, whilst the Lord hung upon the Cross at Calvary, He said " It is finished ;" for His earthly race was run ; His care, toil, weariness, contradiction, sorrow, and suffering were for ever ended.   He had perfectly ful-filled His Father's will, and man had done all that it lay in his power to do.   When our evening shall come, may we feel that through the grace of God our working hours have not been spent in vain.   To a well-spent day the evening becomes a season of—1) Rest.   Toil, activity, busy pursuits are ended at last.   We may have risen early and toiled long ; we may have worked well and learned many a lesson ; our way may have prospered before us, and now has come our hour of rest, grateful alike to body and mind.   2) Peace. Stilled is the turmoil and strife of life ; the eager com-petition ; the contention through which it is ordained that each one shall win their way.   The ship has reached its haven ; storm and billow cease in this quiet water. The end is peace to a life which, blessed by God, has reached its full eventide. 3) Thought. All the events of the past day crowd into the chamber of memory in the evening. Stock is now taken of the profit and loss which the day has produced; of sins committed, or of victories gained over sins ; humiliations and triumphs ; conquests and defeats. O conscience ! be not thou silent, but speak out openly and fearlessly " in the evening of that which is past ;" and mayest thou be able to give a good answer before God.

II. *A Morning.*—This period points to " that which is to come ;" and it is—1) Fresh. A new beginning can be made to-day ; old habits broken through ; new resolutions formed ; the losses of yesterday in some measure atoned for. If life may be likened to a book, then at the beginning of each day a new and a clean page in this book is turned over. The things behind may, in part, be forgotten, and new efforts may be made towards stretching forth to those things which are before. Fresh in mind and body, another day is before us, in which the past may be in great measure redeemed. 2) Untried. " We know not what a day may bring forth ;" it is all unknown. No day exactly repeats itself; no one can ever say, " I feel to-day altogether as I felt yesterday." The experience of each day is, in some respects, peculiar to itself. This fact should teach the caution by which each day in life ought to be ordered. 3) Uncertain. It may never be granted; the last day may not lengthen out " until the evening ; " hence every portion of the day should be turned to its fullest and best account, not a moment of it should be wasted.

III. *A Noon or Mid-day.*—This is the time when the sun is highest in the heavens; when all things are at their height and flow. This fulness of tide and life is typical to thoughtful minds of the day of God— the everlasting day of light and glory. Then should the heart speak " of things sempiternal." This is a time to be—1) Earnestly expected ; bringing with it the perfection of body and soul. 2) Carefully prepared for ; evening and morning wait upon mid-day, as the past and present wait upon the future.

Epilogue.—Sever not by sin the continuity of the day of life. A holy past forms a holy present, and passes onwards to a glorious future; just as the fine sunset promises a fair morn and a beautiful noon.

SERMON XXXII.

SIN.

'' Looking diligently, lest any man fail of the grace of God ; lest
any root of bitterness springing up trouble you.''—*Heb.* xii. 15.

S. Augustine.—'' I know this, that the nature of God
can never fail in any time, point, or portion, whilst
those natures which have been made out of nothing
can do so. The higher the creature, the greater its
failing, if its efficient causes be changed from good to
evil. When the will to sin is present, the guilt is
voluntary, and a just punishment follows from the
voluntary failing ; such fail, not from their evil
natures, but, as against the order of their being, forsaking the highest good for that which is inferior.
Thus : avarice is not the fault of gold, but of man
perversely loving gold, and having forsaken that justice
which ought incomparably to be placed before gold.
Luxury again, is not the fault of fair and of beautiful
bodies, but of a mind perversely loving bodily pleasures,
that temperance being despised, by which we are

joined incorruptibly to fairer and more charming objects. Neither is vainglory the fault of human praise, but of a mind perversely loving to be praised by men, the testimony of conscience being despised. Pride likewise is not the fault of him giving power, or of the power itself, but of a soul perversely loving its power, of the stronger, the more just being scorned. Hence, he who perversely loves good of any kind, even if he obtains it, is evil despite his good, and is wretched as being deprived of what is better."—*De Civ. Dei*, xii. c. viii. vol. v. p. 129, H.

Hence we gain a threefold notion of sin which is many-sided. (Cf. Ser. I. " The Plurality of Sin.") It is—

I. *A Failing.*—A failing of the grace of God which grace—1) restores a lost likeness. We were made in the image and likeness of God. Sin defaced the image and destroyed the likeness; grace removes the stains of sin, and adorns the soul, so that it may become Godlike once more. 2) Grace restores us to God's favour, and unites us with Him Who is our chief good. This chief or highest good the sinner cannot realize; he rests—unhappily—upon a less worthy object. 3) Grace restores our lost inheritance of glory. The sinner works for death and hell, but fails to gain the promised glory. Sin is a failing in all that is best, highest, and holiest.

II. *An Opposition.*—Sin has its root in the opposition of the will of man to the will of God. The will places itself into opposition against God. 1) The affections say, I will love the world rather than God. 2) The reason seeks to remove itself from the domain of faith, in which alone it can find scope for the exercise of all its faculties. 3) The memory, making itself wholly unmindful of God, of His providences, mercies, and judgments.

III. *A Perversion.*—Sweetness is turned to bitterness; light to darkness. Sin is "a root of bitterness," which springing up in the soul perverts all things. 1) Life; 2) Knowledge; 3) Power and energy of every kind; 4) Our nature; which truly belongs to God.

Epilogue.—Sin in act is to be subdued by the root of sin—" the root of bitterness " being rooted out of the heart; and we are bidden to "be perfect." (S. Matt. v. 48.)

SERMON XXXIII.

THE WAY OF HOLINESS.

" An highway shall be there, and a way, and it shall be called the way of holiness."—*Isa.* xxxv. 8.

S. Augustine.—" This our way demands walkers ; but it hates three classes of men : those who stand still, go back, and wander. Of the walkers, some walk more quickly than others, yet both walk. They who stand still must be aroused ; they who go back must be recalled ; they who wander must be led into the way. He who does not advance stands still in the way ; he who goes from what is good to what is evil goes back in the way ; he who forsakes the faith wanders from the way. Who is he, who does not advance ? He who thinks himself to be wise ; who says, ' I am well enough as I am ;' who neglects the Apostolic words : ' Forgetting those things which are behind, and reaching forth unto those things which are before, I press toward the mark for the prize of the high calling of God in Christ Jesus.' (Phil.

iii. 13, 14.) The Apostle confesses that he was running and 'reaching forth;' he stood not still; looked not back; it could not be that he wandered, since he was himself teaching, holding, and showing the way. Who are those who go back? They who return from continency to uncleanness. Such are blamed by the Apostle S. Peter. 'It had been better for them not to have known the way of righteousness,' etc. (2 S. Pet. ii. 21.) Oh! evil deed to look back! 'Remember Lot's wife.' (S. Luke xvii. 32; Gen. xix. 26.) Who are they who wander? The heretics; who, having forsaken the way of truth, are despoiled whilst straying in the desert; who allure souls to sin; and who hinder any one from coming to the heavenly country."—*De Cantico novo*, c. iv. vol ix. p. 277, F.G.

Difficult as it is for us, encompassed as we are with so many and great hindrances—to walk aright along the "highway of holiness;" the "King's highway of the holy Cross;" still we must strive and pray.

I. *Ever to walk onwards.*—Never to remain idle or to be found standing still; duly mindful—1) of that which we have still to do, and of the short time in which so great a work has to be wrought. How many sins have to be subdued; evil habits overcome; fond

desires to be rooted up ?   How many Christian graces
have to be put on ?   How many works "meet for repentance" are yet unfulfilled ?   2) Of the glorious and
great things that are within our grasp, if we will but to
put out our hands and gather them.   "All are yours."
(1 Cor. iii. 22.) Victories over self ; promises of love ;
glimpses of heaven ; and a most blessed sense of pardon
and of peace.   Who can say, "I have exhausted the love,
knowledge, and the grace of God ?"   The highway of
holiness reveals its treasures at every step, and grows
in beauty and pleasantness along each successive
portion of its course.   At the beginning, and at the
beginning only, is it most hard and distressful.

II. *Never to go back.*—Retreat is always humili-
ating ; often it is disgraceful ; always it is ac-
companied by loss.   They who go back on the
"highway of holiness," lose—1) The results of past
life ; former victories over sin ; answers to prayer ;
the fruit of much labour ; hope and heart.   2) "The
answer of a good conscience toward God."   De-
gradation ever waits upon a fall.   The stings of conscience proclaim but too certainly its sense of
cowardice, shame, and defeat.   3) The goal, for
which we had hitherto striven so nobly ; the pearl of
great price ; the unfading crown, and our own soul
beyond all else.

III. *To abide in the way.*—They who go out of

the highway of holiness fall into the bye-ways of—1) superstition. Superstition in this our day is spiritual, not material. Its range is experience, temporal judgment, extraordinary workings of the Holy Ghost, etc. 2) Of unbelief. Of a state in which all revelation is set at nought ; and our relationship with God and the invisible world treated as a vain delusion; or, it may be, as a harmless myth.

Epilogue.—Let your walk in this way be—1) Humble ; 2) Prayerful; 3) Persevering.

SERMON XXXIV.

PARDONED SIN.

" O remember not against us former iniquities."—*Ps.* lxxix. 8.

S. Augustine.—"That pardoned sin can return where brotherly charity is wanting, the Lord most plainly taught in the Gospel in the case of that servant (S. Matt. xviii. 23-35) who when he had been found a debtor to the amount of ten thousand talents, forgave it all at his entreaty. But when he would not have compassion on his fellow-servant who owed him two hundred pence, the lord commanded him to repay that which he had forgiven him."—*De Bapt. Con. Donat.* lib. i. c. xii. vol. vii. p. 34, B.

These words suggest that an answer should be given to the all-important question : Can sin once forgiven by God again be laid to man's charge? Is there such a thing as past sin, which has been once and for ever pardoned? Has the penitent any hope that for him " the former things are passed away ?"

This question has been solved by one whose mind was, both by culture and ability, well fitted to grapple with this solemn consideration, towards the solution of which we follow his guiding. (S. Thomas Aquinas, Summa, 3a. q. 88. 1.) The subject naturally divides itself into—

I. *An Argument.*—That sin once forgiven to the sinner can be again laid to his charge. This view seems to be supported—1) By the parable of the unmerciful servant. (S. Matt. xviii. 23-35.) The new sins of ingratitude to the Lord, and of unforgiveness to the Master, seem to cause the old debt to be brought upon the unmerciful servant. Again: "His Lord delivered him to the tormentors, till he should pay all that was due unto him." Our Blessed Lord then adds as a universal application of this rule, "So likewise," etc. 2) By the parable of the sinful soul "swept and garnished" (S. Luke xi. 24-27), who "taketh seven other spirits more wicked than himself." "This verse," says the Venerable Bede, "is to be feared, not to be explained, lest the sin which we believe to be extinct within us, through our want of care should seize upon us, when we are not watchful." 3) By a statement of the Prophet Ezekiel. (Ezek. xviii. 24.) "When the righteous turneth away from his righteousness . . . all his righteousness that he hath done shall not be mentioned, in his trespass and in his sin:

K

in them shall he die." As if when the penitent sins,
his former repentances and pardons avail him not;
his latter sin brings him under the condemnation of
his former guilt. 4) By the use by S. Paul of the
first verse of the Thirty-second Psalm (Rom. iv. 7),
" whose sins are covered." Grace is said to cover
our sins; by any one deadly sin this covering of grace
is withdrawn, so that our former sins remain all
uncovered again, the sinner being brought under his
old condemnation. From these four passages of Holy
Scripture, many have believed, with S. Augustine, that
sin once pardoned and forgiven by God, is by Him,
upon a fresh transgression, laid again to man's
charge.

II. *An Explanation.*—In deadly sin there are two
elements. Firstly, a turning away from God, which
entails the loss of divine grace and the guilt of eternal
punishment. (S. James ii. 10.) Secondly, a turning
towards the created good, instead of towards God Who
is the uncreated good. It may be that after repentance
we may fall into the very opposite of our old sins;
yet the effect which involves these two conditions is
analogous. These two aspects of sin lead up to the
same result, let the sin itself be of what nature soever
it may. On this principle all these four statements
admit of a ready explanation. 1) In the parable of
the unmerciful servant, the " ten thousand talents "

(£1,875,000) represent the guilt of eternal punishment generally. The unmerciful servant incurred this debt at first by some means which is not mentioned, and afterwards by a cause which is mentioned: combined ingratitude and unforgiveness. These two causes led to the same result. The servant was lost, not by his old debt coming back upon him, but a new debt of like amount for his new offence. 2) In the parable of the chamber swept and garnished (S. Luke xi. 35, 36), it was not the same sin which defiled the man, but a repetition of it; a fresh sin committed after the old habit and manner. 3) On Ezekiel xviii. 24, it may be observed, that by subsequent sin all the merit of former righteousness is lost, but not its effect as an hindrance to further sin. The prophet only asserts by the latter sin, the sinner is brought into a state of guilt; is deprived of the merit of his former holiness; but says not one word about pardoned sin being once more laid to his charge. 4) The expression used by S. Paul from David of "covered" sin (Rom. iv. 7), is a figurative expression. God by His grace hides sin as it were from His eyes, lest He should see it and be obliged to punish it. What God has thus done, remains unchanged and unaltered for ever.

III. *The Conclusion.*—It is hard to believe that the unmerciful servant was "delivered to the tormentors" for his old debt, the same one which had

been pardoned; that the guilt of acts of sin long since
repented of and pardoned, can by a relapse into sin,
be recharged. For—1) The gifts of God are without
repentance (Rom. xi. 29) ; they are not to be recalled.
If pardoned sin could be brought back again, God
would thereby repent of His grace and mercy towards
man. 2) The work of God and His purposes cannot
be thwarted by the work of man. Hence the Apostle's
argument concerning the Jews. (Rom. iii. 3.) 3) An
after act of sin virtually contains the guilt of the
former sin. Fresh sins weigh with an increased weight
upon the pardoned sinner as (Rom. ii. 4, 5), so that
the weight of present sin bears a proportion to the
former pardons. The sentence of the law is propor-
tionately heavier against one who has experienced
former convictions and has paid the full penalty of the
law, in expiation of every such offence.

Epilogue.—1) The joy of a sense of pardoned sin,
should make the soul very careful not to fall once
more into its old state of condemnation. 2) The
gratitude for so many and such infinite pardons should
lead to holiness by the law of love. "How *can* I do
this great wickedness and sin against God ?"

SERMON XXXV.

THE NEW LIFE.

" He that was dead came forth, bound hand and foot with grave-clothes, and his face was bound about with a napkin."—*S. John* xi. 44.

S. Augustine.—"Although we may hold with a full faith the Evangelical narrative of the raising of Lazarus, yet I doubt not that it signifies something by way of allegory ; which allegorizing does not lessen its historic truth. Because S. Paul allegorized the two sons of Abraham (Gal. iv. 22) as the two covenants, it does not follow either that there was not such a person as Abraham, or that he had not two sons.

"Let us therefore consider Lazarus in the tomb to represent, allegorically, a soul buried under the weight of earthly sins—that is, the entire human race, which the Lord in another place (S. Luke xv. 4) compared to a lost sheep—for the liberation of which He said that He had descended, leaving the ninety and nine in the wilderness.

"When the Lord asks 'Where have ye laid him?' I think that He indicated our vocation which is hidden. For the predestination of our calling is hidden, and the interrogation of the Lord, as of one ignorant, is a sign of this secret. The Lord confesses Himself to be ignorant of sinners. (S. Matt. vii. 23.) Hence a like question in Genesis, 'Adam, where art thou?' (Gen. iii. 10) for he had sinned and had hidden himself from the face of God; which hiding is here represented by the tomb; for he who dies is a similitude of him who sins—the buried are hidden from the face of God.

"'Take ye away the stone,' signifies the burden which they of the circumcision wished to lay upon those coming to the Church, against which the Apostle so often testifies; or it may mean the stone of offence caused by those who live badly in the Church.

"'He stinketh, for he hath been dead four days,' the smell of earthly sins and of carnal desires. The body being resolved into dust as the Lord said unto Adam, 'Dust thou art, and unto dust shalt thou return.' (Gen. iii. 19.)

"'Then they took away the stone . . and he that was dead came forth.' This signifies the soul receding

from carnal sins. 'Bound hand and foot with grave
clothes,' bound with unrighteousness; receding from
fleshly things and serving the law of God in the heart,
we are still subject to trouble from the flesh. 'With
the mind I myself serve the law of God; but with the
flesh the law of sin.' (Rom. vii. 25.)

"'His face was bound about with a napkin,' signifying
that in this life we cannot attain unto perfect knowledge. 'Now we see through a glass darkly; but
then face to face.' (1 Cor. xiii. 12.)

"'Jesus saith unto them, Loose him, and let him go;'
that is, that after this life all veils will be taken away
that we may see 'face to face.'

"That there is a great difference between the man
who is tasting the wisdom of God, by Whom we have
been liberated, and others, is indicated by the fact that
except Lazarus came forth he was not unbound. The
renewed soul also, is not able to be freed by the
resolution of the body until it sees the Lord 'through
a glass darkly.' (1 Cor. xiii. 12.) The 'linen clothes
and the napkin' of Him 'Who did no sin,' and was
ignorant of nothing, were found (S. John xx. 5-7)
lying in the tomb. He alone Who was sinless in the
flesh (Isa. liii. 9) was not oppressed in the tomb;

hindered by the grave clothes or blinded by the
' napkin.' "—*Octogint. Quæst.* lxv. vol. iv. p. 219,
G.II.

Coming forth from the tomb of sin, quickened by
repentance and contrition to newness of life, we must
rise with Jesus Christ, and leave our grave-clothes
behind us in the sepulchre.

We must leave behind us—

I. *The old habit of sin.*—The habit of sin bound us
hand and foot whilst we were in the chamber of the
dead: we had no power to stir and to free ourselves.
Sensuality, drunkenness, covetousness, pride, self-will,
etc., had bound us in their iron fetters and they held
us with a giant's strength. God's Spirit is mightier
than Satan; that Holy Spirit has given us the strength
to burst these bonds asunder. Shall we not use this
strength? Being freed from the dominion of sin shall
we live any longer therein? Shall we return again to
the weak and beggarly elements from which we have
been freed?

II. *The associations of sin.*—The occasions of sin
often lead to its committal. We sin from and by
association. Our past misdeeds are frequently asso-
ciated with memories which time and the grave have
alike hallowed. Persons, places, things, are connected
directly or indirectly with some sin; they recall feelings

or acts which we should do well to bury for ever in forgetfulness. "Newness of life," implies newness of association—the forsaking the old associations which have united themselves with so much sin and sorrow. Guard against your special temptation, that is, cut yourself off from the sad memories of the unrepentant and misused past.

III. *The old darkness of sin.*—"Walk as children of the light." "Ye were darkness, now are ye light in the Lord." Scales have, as it were, fallen from your eyes; like the Prodigal, you have "come to yourself," come to see yourself in your true light; to know whither your course of life is tending. Repentance, conversion, quickening of soul, are all so many several forms of enlightenment; are all so many bringings out of the darkness of error into the fulness of saving light and truth. Come forth from the grave of sin with the eyes of your soul wide open: open to the snares and wiles of Satan; open to the infinite mercy, love, and grace of Jesus Christ.

Epilogue.—Freedom is the great prerogative of the Christian; freedom from sin, self, and delusion of every kind. Perfect freedom is the one attribute of the service of Jesus Christ.

SERMON XXXVI.

SELF.

"Are ye not carnal, and walk as men?"—1 *Cor.* iii. 3.

S. Augustine.—" When man lives according to man and not according to God, he is like the devil. Neither can an angel live according to an angel, but according to God, if he would stand in the truth, and speak His truth and not a lie of his own. The Apostle says of man in another place ; ' If the truth of God hath more abounded through my lie.' (Rom. iii. 7.) He contrasts ' my lie,' with ' the truth of God.' When man therefore lives according to the truth, he does not live according to himself, but according to God. It is God who said, ' I am the truth.' (S. John xiv. 6.) When indeed man lives according to himself—that is according to man and not according to God—assuredly he lives according to a lie ; not that man himself is a lie, since God is his Author and Creator—Who is verily, not the author and creator of a lie ; but because man was so rightly created that he should live not according to himself, but according to God by Whom he was made, doing the will of God rather than his own! But not to live as he was created to live is, in itself, a lie. Forsooth, he wishes to be happy, but so living he cannot be happy; for what is more lying than this will? All sin is a lie: it promises what is better; it gives what is worse. God is the source of all blessing to man, who, when he lives according to himself, forsakes God and loses the blessing."—*De Civit. Dei*, lib. xiv. c. 4 vol. v. p. 149, A. B.

When man lives according to himself, his whole life is one long lie. Man is a fallen creature, weak, sinful, and most imperfect; easily led astray, with the heart and the understanding alike darkened. Yet, many live according to themselves: since they—

I. *Rest in themselves*; 1) Being contented with themselves; 2) desiring nothing beyond themselves; 3) feeling no imperfections in themselves. Thousands are in this state; hence all progress is stayed: no endeavour is made to rise to higher and better things. All improvement springs from an intense and humbling feeling of our own imperfection. We feel that we are wanting in something, therefore we make every effort to supply our deficiency. True for the best things of all. Until we have ceased to rest in ourselves, we shall never seek to rest upon the Holy Person and the finished work of Jesus Christ. The infinite need of something without us to complete our shortcomings and to do for us what we cannot do for ourselves, is the ground of all earnest seeking after; holiness, goodness, and the likeness to Jesus Christ. God as being perfect rests in Himself. For man being imperfect, to rest in Himself is for Him to "live according to man, and not according to God."

II. *Measure all things by themselves.*—They who live "according to man," measure all things by their own standard; and limit their views to the horizon of their own knowledge or experience. They are "a law unto themselves." Such measurement must be—1) Partial: favouring all that coincides with our own notions. 2) Imperfect: founded upon a one-sided view of the case. 3) Arrogant: leading a man to set up himself as a judge and a final court of appeal.

III. *Become the slaves of man.*—Living "according to man," is living in all the lusts and appetites of a fallen and a corrupt nature; is living "after the flesh." It implies a giving place to—1) All the evil thoughts of the soul: hatred, pride, covetousness, and the like. 2) All the lesser desires of the body: luxury, sloth, sensuality, drunkenness, and the other evil passions. Habits of indulgence are as fetters and chains, whether laid upon soul or body.

Epilogue.—Rather let us live " according to God."
1) Resting in God, in submission, faith, etc. 2)
Measuring all things by His standard. 3) Living
according to His holy rule of life.

SERMON XXXVII.

FAITH.

" Increase our faith."—*S. Luke* xvii. 5.

S. Augustine.—" There are three classes of things credible; one includes those things which are ever believed and never understood; such is the entire range of history, embracing temporal events and human actions. The second class contains those things which are both believed in and understood; such are mathematical and other exercises of the pure reason. Lastly, there are those things which are first believed and are afterwards understood. Of this nature is divine truth, which can only be understood by those who keep the commandments in a pure heart, and who are accepted for their holy lives."— *Octogint. Quæst.* xlviii. vol. iv. p. 211, A.

In one sense there is not, nor has there ever been, any lack of faith upon the earth. In every age men have been found to be "too superstitious." There is a belief or faith of devils, which brings fear and dark-

ness in its train; there is a saving faith which brings
love and gladness to the soul.

Our faith or belief is threefold. In the—

I. *Unintelligible.*—Such are the things which are
believed in, but which cannot be understood. We
live in a world of mystery, and we are in ourselves a
mystery unto ourselves. Life and death are both
mysteries. Why was I born to die? Why was a
soul which is capable of looking before and after,
wrapped up in a body which is so strictly limited to
time and space? The world of nature without me, I
see it, I cannot but believe in it, yet I cannot understand it. Have the brutes a soul? Who knows? I
cannot but believe in the wild and wilful course of
man, as chronicled in the course of history; the rise
and fall of nations, kingdoms, systems of theology and
philosophy, moral and physical. The wayward
workings of man's unruly will are stamped over all
this world of ours, and yet we cannot understand its
impulses. As moral, intellectual, Christian people,
we live in the midst of wonders which we are bound
to believe in, although we cannot explain them. Yes!
there is faith enough in the world and in the world's
ways.

II. *The Intelligible and Credible.*—Such are the
things which are both believed in and understood.
The very mention of such things is a vindication of

the nobility of our nature, which asserts its acceptance of certain truths which cannot be rejected without transgressing the plain and rigorous laws of thought. Hence studies like arithmetic, mathematics, and logic, are valuable as uniting faith with reason; they present conclusions which demand the mind's acceptance as being proved by the undoubted testimony of the reason.

III. *The Credible and Unintelligible.*—Such are the things which are believed in first, and are to be understood afterwards. They embrace the whole body of revealed truth. It is accepted because it comes from God. It is—1) a discipline; 2) a purification; 3) an endowment. We discipline our hearts by a humble reception of it. Having received it, it gradually purifies the heart and life. With the purification there comes a spiritual enlightenment—a teaching by the Spirit of God which leads us into domains into which reason at present is powerless to follow.

Epilogue.—Lord, "increase our faith" in the highest truth; since such increase must become our eternal gain.

SERMON XXXVIII.

PREACHING.

"If any man speak, let him speak as the oracles of God."
—1 *S. Pet.* iv. 11.

S. Augustine.—" He who endeavours by preaching
to persuade to what is good, prays and aims that he may
teach, delight, and move ; despising none of these three,
so that he may be heard intelligently, willingly, and
obediently. He that so speaks aptly and conveniently,
not undeservedly can be called eloquent, although he
may not carry the assent of his audience. The author
of Roman eloquence [Cicero] seemed to allude to these
three qualifications when he said, 'He is an orator
who can say small things softly ; middling things
temperately ; great things grandly.' He therefore
will be eloquent who, in order to teach, can say
humble truths gently ; to delight, can say moderate
things temperately ; to move or bend, great things
grandly."—*De Doc. Christianâ*, lib. iv. c. xvii. vol.
iii. p. 31, D.

I.   L

Sermons are often dull and profitless because they are wanting in these three elements of teaching, pleasing, and bending or moving men's hearts, properly combined and present in a due proportion. These three qualities are present in the ' oracles,' or discourses of God which—

I. *Teach.*—In this world and life we ought to be as children at school, ever learning ; ever ready to receive instruction since we are ever needing it. The understanding cries out for food : "Give me knowledge and instruction." The pulpit is a teaching place in which is taught—1) Duty : moral, social, and Christian. 2) Knowledge of divine things : of the Holy Scriptures ; their histories ; their meanings ; their testimonies to the faith. 3) Doctrine ; which enables us to accept the entire Rule of Faith, and to reject all novelties in religion. That heavenly teaching by which the mind of Jesus Christ comes down to, and holds converse with, our own feeble and imperfect minds. Teaching—1) Informs : it reduces the soul to order and form, and changes its natural chaos into a spiritual world of harmony. 2) Edifies or builds up : taking the rough stones and material of the mind, and working them up into "an habitation of God through the Spirit." 3) Adorns : all knowledge is a garniture of the soul ; it does for the mind that which comely and well-ordered apparel does for the body. The untaught soul is clad in the rags and tatters of opinion, conceit, and prejudice, instead of in the whole and perfect garment of that knowledge which is humbly and thankfully received as from the hand of God. Every Sunday ought to convey some morsel of knowledge to the understanding of the hearer, which will abide in and exercise a wholesome and saving action upon the soul all throughout the following week.

II. *Please.*—The oracles of God delight and please —1) By their endless variety of subjects. There is no monotony in Holy Scripture; which is more diversified than the most varied landscape which our earth affords. Each inspired penman leaves his own distinct individuality upon his own page. The preacher must ever change his theme, ever present the old truth in a new light; the same unchangeable Figure (i.e. Jesus,) clad in different garments. 2) By their illustrations. Spiritual lessons are taught in so many ways in Holy Scripture : by history; by type; by parable; by discourse ; by songs ; by prayers. The preacher should press into his service any event or saying which is worthy of record, which avails to illustrate his subject. 3) By their adaptations and applications. The "oracles of God " speak with a human voice, appealing to human feeling; supplying human needs with their divine help. The preacher must adapt and apply all his teaching to the hearts and consciences of his hearers.

III. *Move or Bend.*—Holy Scripture often moves the heart to—1) Repentance for past sin; 2) Confession and contrition for present sin; 3) Holy resolutions of amendment of life against future sin. Preaching is in vain, if it leads no souls to holiness, and if it excites no desires in men's minds to attain unto the higher life which belongs to the children and friends of God.

Epilogue.—These needs in the preacher imply corresponding needs in the hearer, who must be—1) apt to learn; 2) ready to listen with pleasure; 3) disposed to be excited to holiness. He must be, in short, intelligent, willing, and obedient, ever looking to receive a blessing from the mouth of the preacher.

SERMON XXXIX.

THE SPIRIT'S WORK.

" Thy Spirit is good."—*Ps.* cxliii. 10.'

S. Augustine.—" As therefore no one is rightly wise ; rightly understands, prevails rightly in counsel and might ; no one is knowingly pious ; or piously knowing, no one fears God with a chaste fear, except he shall have received the spirit of wisdom and understanding of counsel and might, of knowledge and piety, and fear of the Lord ; (Isa. xi. 2) ; nor has any one true virtue ; sincere charity ; continent religion ; save by the spirit of virtue, charity, and continence ; so, without the spirit of faith, no one can rightly believe ; savingly pray, without the spirit of prayer. After one manner He helps not as yet indwelling ; after another manner, indwelling. For not yet indwelling, He helps that they may become faithful ; indwelling, He helps them as being faithful."—*Contra Pelagianos*, Epist. cv. vol. ii. p. 157, G.

" The Holy Spirit works within [intrinsecus] as a medicine which is used without [extrinsecus] may do good."—*De Civitate Dei*, lib. xv. c. 6. vol. v. p. 161, H.

Without the Holy Spirit moved upon the waters of man's soul, " which are without substance," (Confess. lib. xiii. c. 7); we should be—

I. *Dead.*—Sin is death. The Holy Ghost being sinless is life (S. Amb.); and He raises us from the death of sin to the life of righteousness. He gives us a new birth, which involves a new nature. ' Ye must be born again." (S. John. iii. 17.) The life which the Spirit gives us in exchange for the darkened life of our lowly nature, is a life which is—1) Immortal : never to be swallowed up in death ; never to be subjected to the powers of darkness. Our mortality after the flesh, throws its sombre shadow over the highest and fairest scenes of this present state of being This new life is never to collapse into the sad state of nothingness. 2) Godlike : hence holy, happy glorious, expansive ; rejoicing in its very being; exulting over the conscious exercise of its powers. 3) Rudimentary : here on earth, like the life of a little child amongst men; all undeveloped ; and all imperfect ; yet giving abundant promise of a future spring-time and a golden summer, and a glorious harvest.

II. *Unpardoned.*—If all the richest blessings of life were strewn about our paths, houses, friends, means of every kind in unlimited luxuriance ; and yet the shadow of a known and coming agony cast its gloom over all ; if the sword of Damocles was hanging over our heads, each blessing would seem to be a mockery of goodness. The unpardoned soul carries a burden vast and heavy to bear about with it wherever it goes ; a sense of weariness and oppression ; of hopelessness and helplessness, which robs the brightest hours of their charm. The Holy Spirit intercedes for pardon (Rom. viii. 26) ; and so removes the burden ; drives back the shadow ; and places a glorious future before the soul.

III. *Uninspired.* — I speak not of the extra-ordinary gifts of inspiration, such as fall to the lot of prophets, saints, seers, and apostles ; but of an inspiration ; an excitation, an arousing and a quickening, by which the Holy Spirit is wont to work upon and within the souls of men. Inspiring souls —1) to seek for light and knowledge ; 2) to endure heroically ; 3) to love eternally ; 4) to live holily.

Epilogue.—1. May those who know not as yet His blessed Presence, remember how He is even now yearning over them. 2 May those who acknowledge His gracious indwelling go on in His might from strength to strength and " from glory to glory, as by the Spirit of the Lord."

SERMON XL.

KNOWLEDGE.

"Knowledge is pleasant unto the soul."—*Prov.* iii. 10.

S. Augustine.—" *Reason.*—What therefore do you desire to know ? *Augustine.*—All these things themselves that I have prayed for. *R.*—Briefly enumerate them. *A.*—I desire to know God and the soul. *R.*—Nothing more ? *A.*—Nothing truly."—*Soliloq.* lib. i, c. 2, vol i. p. 197, E.

It is almost saddening to consider the infinite variety of knowledge that exists in the world, and how small a portion of this vast wealth it is possible for any one mind to master and appropriate to its own use. After a long lifetime spent upon one department of learning, how superficial and imperfect is the mastery acquired over it; and then what hundreds of other branches of information are left uncared for. The greatest, the most highly gifted mind, can only acquire an infinitesimal portion of a great whole. What is to be done then ? Because the whole is beyond man's power, is therefore no attempt to be made to gain the possible moiety ? Rather select out of the great storehouse that which is of the highest value, and endeavour to make that well-chosen portion of knowledge your very own.

Such a selection was made by one of the greatest of Christian thinkers of the olden time ; by one who was variously learned in the departments of study which were extant in his day ; and he, forsaking all the others, was content to limit his acquisition of knowledge to that of God, His nature, attributes, and works ; and of his own soul, with its several functions, affections, appetites, and capacities. The former knowledge is a revelation, either of the Revealed Word without man ; or of the Spirit of God within man. The latter, flows from self-examination and self-communion ; from a deep and earnest communing with the heart, from the searching examination and proving of self. Amidst the many branches of knowledge open to man, why did this great Father and thinker select these two especially ? Because, upon examination, such knowledge will be found to be of all branches of learning the most—

I. *Perfect.*—1) In subject. God is perfection ; He is the only perfect being whom it is permitted man to study. The mind of man, being made after God's image and likeness, is the next perfect object of study. The study of the perfect invites to and interests the

soul in Him Who said to man, " Be ye perfect, even
as your Father Which is in Heaven is perfect." 2) In
means. God must be known "—*a*) by His revelation,
which is perfect in truth, holiness, and in His other
attributes ; *b*) By His works, which are " perfect in
beauty." Man must be known by the exercise of
pure thought, which is freed from the desires and the
false impressions of the senses.

II. *Profitable.*—Knowledge of God and the soul
avails—1) For this present life : guiding and pro-
tecting the path of life ; teaching man both his
stren th and his weakness ; leading him to forsake
the lower and to aim at the higher life ; bringing forth
much present fruit ; inasmuch as God blesses prudent
endeavour and holy resolve, and ripens them into
deeds, "meet for repentance." 2) In the life to
come : preparing the mind for the fulness of the
revelation which will fall to the lot of the sons of God
hereafter. Profitable : carrying a double blessing
with us of the life which now is and of that which
shall be.

III. *Satisfying.*—As the mind of man is a counter-
part of the mind of God, which is infinite, it cannot
be satisfied and rest contented in finite things.
God is the fulness of light to the understanding ; of joy
to the memory ; of power to the will ; of love to the
affections. God satisfies the soul because He is—1)

Infinite—2) True. 3) Perfect. The soul in an inferior sense satisfies itself, since it cannot go beyond its own conceptions, desires and imaginings. Hence there is a rest to be gained from the knowledge of God and the soul.

IV. *Eternal.*—All other branches of knowledge, however good and valuable, are merely temporal, this alone is eternal. It concerns—1) Immortal natures : God and the soul. 2) Immortal condition and states of being : heaven and the heavenly life. We gain a knowledge in time which is to be perfected in eternity.

Epilogue.—Place this twofold knowledge before all other learning, and the fruit it will yield will correspond to its own several attributes.

SERMON XLI.

PERFECTION.

" Let us, therefore, as many as be perfect, be thus minded."
—*Phil.* iii. 15.

S. Augustine.—" Yet, just before uttering these words, the Apostle had confessed his imperfection, ' not as though I were already perfect.' Thou canst only be perfect here by knowing that thou canst not be perfect here. This, therefore, will be thy perfection to pass by one, to hasten to another, acknowledging that all being done, there is still something more to be attained. I call myself, therefore, imperfect and perfect; imperfect, as having not yet received that which I wish ; perfect, because I know what is still wanting to me."—*Enarr. in Psalmum* xxxviii. vol .viii. p. 122. D. p. 123, A.

All truly great and humble minds have longed to fulfil the Lord's command, "Be ye perfect " (S. Matt. v. 48); and feeling bitterly how far they have fallen

below their ideal standard, they long for the time
when perfection shall have come, and all that is "in
part" shall for ever be done away with." (1 Cor.
xiii. 10.)

That perfection—the germs of which only can be
attained in this life—consists of four conditions of
being, which all should seek as far as possible to
realize. These conditions are essential to the perfect
development of our moral and spiritual being.

I. *To know nothing but the truth.*—A large portion
of that imperfection which produces so much of the
misery and sin of the world, comes from men walking
in the uncertain paths of error and deceit. They miss
the way of truth ; they gain opinion, which is selfish,
false, and partial; and thus they lose all real knowledge of God, His Church, His grace, and His means
of salvation ; of themselves, their strength, and their
weakness, the purpose and end of their lives. Of how
many who are still tied and bound by the chain of sin,
and who have never risen to the higher life, may
it be said, "The way of truth they have not
known."

II. *To desire nothing but happiness.*—All desire
happiness in some form or other, but few desire true
happiness. The happiness which is to be desired is—
1) Satisfying : leaving no wish unfulfilled, no capacity
empty. As long as one small craving remains, happi-

ness must be considered to be imperfect.   2) Lasting : not an enjoyment for to-day to pass away to-morrow, leaving blankness and desolation behind it.   Ephemeral happiness is imperfect, for a sense of its coming deprivation tinges it with a certain sorrow.   3) Progressive ; increasing with the capacity for its reception. That which is sufficient for happiness to a soul of one capacity, would leave an aching void in another of higher culture or of keener feeling.

III. *To feel nothing but love.*—The heavenly life is a life of perfect love.   All forms of the unloving ; of hate ; envy; selfishness, etc., disturb the soul and mar its perfection.   Love fixes the soul upon—1) God Who "is love" and unchangeable.   The author of every blessing.   2) Man, in his best and noblest points, with many of his weaknesses and imperfections covered.   3) All that is true and good and beautiful in every relation of life, in every creation of the mind.   God, Who is perfection, is also love ; and the perfect nature is one of infinite capabilities of loving.

IV. *To work nothing but holiness.*—Sin, whether of the thought or deed, destroys perfection, since it brings loss, punishment, and unhappiness in its train. Sin makes man too imperfect for heaven; too imperfect to fulfil his due and proper work upon earth.   Sin is a disturbance of the equilibrium of perfection.

Epilogue.—The Lord Jesus Christ, as the Perfect

Man, came to lead us to this perfection; to be our truth, our happiness, and eternal salvation, our loving brother, our source of holiness. In Him we find our own future perfection prophetically personified.

SERMON XLII.

THE PATH OF DUTY.

"Fear not, Zacharias, for thy prayer is heard, and thy wife
Elizabeth shall bear thee a son."—*S. Luke* i. 13.

S. Augustine.—" It is not likely that Zacharias—
who was a righteous man, and old in experience and
years—when he was offering for the sins of the people,
for their salvation and redemption, whilst, too, they
all were waiting for His offering—that he, an old man,
having an aged wife, leaving the public intercession,
would pray that he might receive children. Hitherto
he had despaired of offspring, and now he disbelieved
the angelic message. ' Whereby shall I know this ?'
The sign of dumbness was vouchsafed (S. Luke i.
20), which signified that prophecy lacked an intelligible sound, that it was not understood until it was
fulfilled by the Lord. What said the Angel to him ?
' Thy prayer is heard.' His prayer for the people ;
whose salvation and redemption, and the abolition of
whose sins was about to be wrought by Christ. To

I.   M this end was the son to be born, announced to Zacharias, because the child was destined to be the precursor of Christ."—*Quæstiones Evangelicæ*, lib. i. 21. vol. iv. p. 130, C.

The unselfish, strict discharge of duty always brings a blessing with it. To do or to suffer is in itself healthful, when duty calls us to one or other of these lots. In the case of Zacharias the reward for his unselfish following of the path of duty was :—

I. *Unexpected.*—All hope and expectation of being blessed in his issue had long since died away with him. There was a time when he thought that it might be his happy lot to possess a son who should carry on his name and office when he was gathered to his fathers ; but that time had now passed by long since. Resignation had succeeded expectation. The just and calm fulfilment of the duties of life, and a due preparation for his coming end, were now his thought and care. In fulfilling his duty, he entertained an Angel unawares; and the prayer of long-gone-by days, the yearnings of his youth and spring-time, were alike to be answered now. An unexpected blessing, light, and joy, was to be his portion. When we are walking in the way of duty, humbly, stedfastly, unselfishly before God, then the unexpected help, and comfort, and blessing comes. When the sacrifice of all that is dear is to be offered at the shrine of obedience, the eyes are opened, and the ram is seen holden in a thicket by its horns. (Gen. xxii. 13.)

II. *Grateful.*—No gift was so precious to the Jew as that of posterity. Riches and honours, the highest advancement in life, Zacharias would gladly have sacrificed to gain a son. The birth of an heir fulfilled the long desire of a life. A child was the one thing wanting to complete his happiness. God, therefore, rewarded him for his honest discharge of duty in the way of all others, which was acceptable to him. So was Ruth gratefully blessed for remaining with Naomi.

III. *Bountiful.*—Duty ought to claim no recompense, for man can never perfectly fulfil it; and the testimony of a good conscience is a sufficient remuneration for all toil, suffering, and sacrifice of self. God ever rewards the true and faithful by blessings manifold, which are far beyond their merits; for godliness hath the twofold promise of this world and the next. Small service, performed from right motives, never fails of an overflowing blessing. Joseph is exalted and enriched for interpreting Pharaoh's dream, instead of refusing in anger so to do.

Epilogue.—Shrink not from the path of duty, be it ever so hard, ever so rugged. The reward will surely come sooner or later. In due time you shall reap if you faint not.

SERMON XLIII.

JESUS SLEEPING.

"He was asleep."—*S. Matt.* viii. 24.

S. Augustine.—"We sail through a certain sea, and winds and gales are not wanting; our ship is well nigh filled with the daily temptations of this world. Whence is this, save that Jesus sleeps? But what is it for Jesus to sleep? Thy faith which is in Jesus has slept. The storms of this sea arise; you behold the evil to prosper, the good to toil; it is a trial; it is a wave; and thy soul exclaims, 'O God, is this really Thy righteousness, that the wicked should flourish and the good should toil.' You say to God, 'Is this Thy righteousness?' And God says to you, 'Is this thy faith?' Have I promised you these things? Was it for this that you became a Christian, that you should prosper in this world, and that in the future you should be miserably tormented in hell? Here the wicked flourish who afterwards will be tormented with the devil. Why do you speak thus? Wherefore are you disturbed by the waves and tempest of the sea? It is because Jesus is sleeping, because your faith in Jesus is asleep in your heart? What do you do that you may be delivered? Awake Jesus and say, ' Lord, we perish !' The uncertainties of the sea move us, ' we perish.' He will watch, that is, He restores your faith to you, and He assisting, you will consider in your heart that what is given to the wicked only, will not remain with them, for it will forsake them living or be forsaken by them dying; but that which is promised to you will remain for ever."—*Enarr. in Psal.* xxv. vol. viii. p. 44. H.

The Presence of Jesus Christ, which He gives to every one who is baptized into His name, is a Presence which is of infinite value for this present life, as well as our only security for the life to come. When this Presence is not realized; has no hold or action upon the soul; then Jesus is surely sleeping in the ship of the soul. When Jesus Christ is sleeping we lose—

I. *Faith.*—The storm of doubt carries us hither and thither; our creed changes with the moon. We are seeking to navigate a difficult and most treacherous sea without either compass or chart; and the clouds of doubt above the head prevent any observations being taken to learn the course. Doubt leads to error; error to destruction. Shipwreck is imminent. The rocks and breakers are around and hem us in. "Lord, save us, we perish."

II. *Love.*—It is love that lightens care and toil. There is neither care nor toil for the beloved object; they are swallowed up in a higher feeling, which casts its care upon the loved one and toils with a ready will and a light heart which is gladdened by sympathy. When love dies out, care presses down the soul; the waters are coming in. "Lord, save us, we perish."

III. *Hope.*—When we lose hope, the waves of sorrow sadly buffet us. With hope as a companion we ride upon the cresting billows, triumphant and rejoicing. When hope is lost, we sink under the waters of sorrow; we are swallowed up by over much sorrow. "Lord, save us, we perish."

IV. *Obedience.*—The tempest of sin, with its gales of temptation, tears our sails, breaks our spars, and drives us before it at its most cruel mercy. The pilot is sleeping; the rudder-bands are loose; all is dismay, lawlessness, and in a confusion which must end in death. "Lord, save us, we perish."

Epilogue.—Keep Jesus waking in the soul, by ever earnestly thinking upon, praying to, and referring all things to Him.

SERMON XLIV.

HAPPINESS.

"We call the proud happy."—*Mal.* iii. 15.

S. Augustine.—"Assuredly all men desire to live happily, neither is there any one of the human race who would not agree to this sentiment almost before it were fully spoken. But in my opinion, I cannot call that man happy who has not that which he loves, whatsoever thing it may be : neither he who has that which he loves, if it be harmful; nor he who does not love what he has if it be the best. For he who desires that which he cannot obtain is tormented ; and he who has gained that which he does not desire is deluded; and he who does not desire that which can be gained is sick. None of these men are happy. The fourth case remains as I see it, in which the happy life can be found, when that which is the best for man is both loved and possessed."—*De Mor. Eccles.* lib. i. ciii. vol. i. p. 287, A.

Mistakenly then, we call the proud happy; and not
the proud alone, but the noble, the wealthy, the
honourable, and the beautiful. We confound happiness
with what seems to be a prosperous or successful lot
in life. We confuse some of the means of happiness
with the end which is joy and contentment of heart.
True happiness is an inward feeling; it can only proceed from the state of the mind, and not from any
outward or bodily circumstances of life. We learn
that true happiness consists in a state which is—

I. *Satisfied.*—To be perfectly happy we must be
perfectly satisfied—we must possess that which we
both love and desire. No unfulfilled longing can find
any place in a soul which is perfectly happy. Longing
implies incompletion, whilst completion is the very
basis of happiness. They only are happy who have
that which supplies their every longing. As we are
immortal, spiritual, and sympathetic natures, the
object of our love and our fruition must be—1) Immortal; never to perish with the using thereof, or
capable of separation from us. 2) Spiritual; other-
wise it cannot appeal to our highest and best faculties,
it cannot fill up the void in a nature which is itself
Spiritual and Godlike. 3) Sympathetic; as so to
answer to the thousand pleadings of the soul that
seeks for sympathy and love. The loved object must
have certain fixed relations with the one who loves;

and it must be " that which is the best for man " to possess.

II. *Safe.*—The gratification of any harmful desire cannot confer pleasure. Men often look for happiness in the indulgence of the lower appetites of both body and soul; in a course of sensuality, avarice, ambition, and the like; and they obtain their end, which wholly cheats them when it is gained. Sin is an offence against the law of our being—physical, moral, spiritual; all things harmful are sinful; so that the acquirement of a harmful possession is a rebellion against the law of life, and as such must necessarily bring, not happiness, but sorrow and misery in its train. Things harmful cause—1) Remorse for the past; 2) Discontent for the present; 3) Fear for the future. With these three elements at work within the soul, where is the room for happiness ?

III. *Appetitive.*—The finest food is of no avail to that body whose power of enjoying meats and drinks is lost. Nothing can bring pleasure to a soul that has lost its appetite for enjoyment. Heaven will realize the fulness of the appetitive faculty with its ample fulfilment. All the flowers of the universe would be valueless to the bee without the desire and power to appropriate their honey. The power to possess is implied in the happiness of possession. This appetitive faculty which is essential to true happiness implies

—1) An ardent longing; 2) A vigorous application; 3) An entire assimilation. This happiness is a sign of spiritual health; since " he who does not desire that which can be gained is sick."

Epilogue.—Happiness implies three factors—a longing; a good thing longed for; and a perfect sense of satisfaction in its possession. The truly happy are they who long after holiness as including both faith and knowledge—the greatest and most enduring good—and who find therein the completion of their nature; the fulfilment of their every desire.

SERMON XLV.

THE NIGHT.

"The night is far spent."—*Rom.* xiii. 12.

S. Augustine.—"Night is that humility where there is the sorrow of mortality; it is night in the proud doing very unjustly; night in the weariness, from sinners leaving the law of God; lastly, it is night in the place of this pilgrimage."—*Enarr. In Psalm.* cxviii. vol. iii. p. 490, C.

Night is then morally representative of a state of imperfection which mainly flows from mortality, injustice, sin, and change. The present life is one long night, save when it is enlightened by the shining in upon it of the rays of the " Sun of Righteousness." The future in glory will be one long day. " Sorrow may endure for the night " of this world, but "joy cometh in the morning," in the day of the Paradise of God. The conditions then of this moral night are—

I. *Mortality.*—"The sorrow," or wretchedness, of mortality " brings humility in its train; not that humility alone which results from an entire submission to the Divine will, but that kind of humility which flows from a crushing sense of defeat. For mortality—1) Weakens life, and curtails its power, since death comes in to stay both man's work and progress. Had there been no mortality, the good might have gone on to almost infinite goodness, knowledge, and rule ; and the punishment of evil would have been more fully, than it now is, worked out in this world. Whilst now, but few mature years are allotted to man, and then the humility of helplessness and loss of faculty stays his course, and he sinks gradually out of sight. 2) Frustrates : it does not allow a full and perfect end to any work and labour under the sun. Life is but a seedtime, the harvest of which must be gathered in by others. 3) Discourages : all work in the world seems to be performed against such tremendous opposition. The worker may at any moment be called from his work, and become as if he had never been. Yes, mortality is truly night; a seeing through a glass darkly ; with the dark cloud of un-certainty ever hanging veiled.

II. *Injustice.*—·Every form of injustice darkens the conscience. Injustice darkens—1) The doer : until by habit, might becomes right, and the law of doing unto others as they would we should do unto us a dead letter. Habitual injustice completely blunts the moral sense. The reflex action of sin upon the sinner,

is a direr evil than sin itself. 2) The sufferer : injustice turns peace into turmoil ; joy into sorrow ; and
darkens life, by depriving it of its due and lawful
elements. Life is ever dark under a great wrong. 3)
The indifferent : the looker on who sees wickedness
flourishing, and truth and goodness depressed ; who
sees injustice stalking boldly before men, becomes of
darkened faith, and loses his hold upon the spiritual
world.

III. *Sin.*—All the real moral and spiritual light in
this world is but the pale reflection of the glory and
holiness of the world which is out of sight, proceeding
from Him Who is the fountain of light. Sin inter-
cepts these rays of Divine light as they are proceeding
to enlighten the soul ; it casts its own dark shadow
between the soul and the light of God ; and in proportion as the sin becomes deadly, so does the night
become dark. This night of sin is—1) Terrible : as
the Egyptian ninth plague. 2) Dangerous : for in it
the soul cannot see its secret enemies, the right
way, and the dangers in the path of life. 3) Unprofitable : no work can be done in utter darkness.
" The unfruitful works of darkness." (Eph. v. 11.)
4) Solitary : since sin robs the soul of all true love
and friendship.

IV. *Pilgrimage.*—" It is night in the place of this
pilgrimage," since this world leads onwards to the

next, just as night leads on to day. This life, as being a pilgrimage towards heaven, may be said to be night, because it is—1) Imperfect: " Now we see through a glass, darkly." 2) Changing : even as the night changes to the day, so does the night of time change into eternity. 3) This world is both a shadowy and dreamlike life, for the " fashion of it passeth away."

Epilogue.—Turn the night of this world and life. O turn ye to the light of Holy love, truth, and goodness ; even to Jesus Christ, Who " is the true light, which lighteth every man coming into this world." He will make all your darkness to be light, and in this light shall ye see light. In the day of God there will be immortality, righteousness, holiness, and an eternal home.

SERMON XLVI.

GOD.

"O God, Thou art my God."—*Ps.* lxiii. 1.

S. Augustine.—" O God, the true and highest life, by Whom, through Whom, and in Whom all live, who live truly and blessedly. God, from Whom to be estranged is to fall, and to Whom to be turned is to arise, in Whom to remain is to be. God, Whom no one loses unless deceived; no one seeks unless admonished ; no one finds unless cleansed. God, Whom to know is to live ; Whom to serve is to reign ; Whom to praise is salvation and joy to the soul. Thee I praise, bless, and adore, with heart and lips and all my powers."—*Meditat.* cxxxii. vol. ix. p. 305, F.

Such a God could David claim to be his; and we as His sons, by our new birth, can more truly claim to be ours. Do we make good our claim ? A needful question, since there are some who—

I. *Lose God.*—Sad thought, God was mine once. Long ago I loved Him, rejoiced in Him, tried to obey

Him and to know more of Him. Now I have lost Him: I am living without God in the world. I did not mean to lose Him, it was not a wilful loss; but I was beguiled and deceived into losing Him. I was deceived for—1) My mind was blinded. I could not see things as they really are. The light of heaven, of revelation, of God's truth and Presence was darkened within me. Blindfolded was I led by the devil captive to him at his will. 2) My affections were perverted. I loved that which I ought to have hated, and I hated that I ought to have loved. I placed my soul upon a foundation which was worthless and perishable—sowing to the whirlwind to reap the storm. 3) My talents were prostituted. I turned against God my time, my thoughts, my speech, the whole endeavour of my life. I was compelled to sin; I was living as if under a spell. Oh! fearful state!

II. *Seek God.*—There are seekers after God—if haply they might find Him—in every age; earnest, fervent seekers after Him; knowing no rest until they can say, "Abba, Father," "O God, Thou art my God." Such seekers are admonished by the voice of —1) Conscience. Conscience is God's witness of Himself in the soul; it never lets the godless have rest; it is ever bearing witness against them in reproaches, regrets, self-accusations, and self-con-demnations. 2) Providence. "There are it may be so many voices in the world, and none of them without signification." (1 Cor. xiv. 10.) Providence, in the way of unexpected blessings and severe trial. 3) Of God Himself speaking by the mouth of His Priests, His Word, His Sacraments, and the Services of His Church.

III. *Find God.*—Not all who seek God, find Him. Some seek Him carelessly or despairingly, for themselves, with no feeling of love for Him, or honour of His Name. We must be cleansed from all impurity of the flesh and of the spirit, if we would hope to find Him. (2 Cor. vii. 1.) We must—1) Resist habitual sin; 2) Pray and strive against occasional sin; 3) Be adorned with the graces of holiness, love, and fear.

Epilogue.—In losing God, all is lost, earth and heaven. In seeking God, there is a discipline and a reward. The gaining God conveys the fulness of blessing.

I   N

SERMON XLVII.

FAITH A TEACHER.

" Your father Abraham rejoiced to see My day : and he saw it and was glad."—*S. John.* viii. 56.

S. Augustine.—" It is faith to believe that which you not yet see; it is the reward of this faith to see that which you believe. In the time of faith, therefore, as in the time of sowing, let us not fail, and to the end let us not fail, but let us persevere until we reap that which we have sown."—*De Verb. Apost.* Ser. xxvii. vol. x. p. 129, G.

The cultivation of many of the arts and sciences, may be said to so develope the senses of touch, sight, and hearing, that they may be almost considered to have been created during the process of technical education. All definite and real study in like manner, so draws out and strengthens the powers of the mind, that in due time, it seems to have become the recipient of almost supernatural gifts. Hence the vast difference

which is to be found between the educated and the
ignorant in their perceptive faculties of both body and
mind. As there are earthly teachers of mark and
value, both for the development and purification of
man, so faith can be considered to be essentially the
heavenly teacher, leading the mind into regions which
are not contradictory to, but which are simply beyond
the ken and the domain of reason. As an element of
justification, faith is a state, a condition which is both
passive and quiet; as a teaching factor it is most active and successful. It acts as a Divine intuition,
bringing down heaven to earth; the mind of God to
the mind of man. Faith opens the book of God;
His revelation; His providence; His grace; in the
same way; although in an infinitely higher degree;
that education opens the book of nature. Now
education is the product of thought, care, discipline,
toil, and bodily denial; and faith is likewise the
product of prayer, meditation, holiness, love, and repentance, all combined. We spare no pains to gain
the key by which we may unlock the knowledge of
that which relates to time. What study and care
do we give in order to obtain the key which unlocks
the knowledge of eternity? As a citizen of the world,
no one can afford to slight education. As a citizen of
the kingdom of God, no one can live without faith,
which both teaches us, and applies to us the mind

and will of God. God cannot be known now, save by faith, and unless He be known, He cannot be obeyed and loved ; hence, " without faith, it is impossible to please Him." (Heb. xi. 6.) Words, sermons, instructions, etc., are all so many pedagogues, or leaders, to the school of Jesus Christ, but the true teacher in that school is faith. How does faith teach ? By way of revelation or vision to the soul; which vision is—

I. *Prophetic.*—It enabled Abraham to look over a chasm of two thousand years. A longing to penetrate into the secrets of the future, pertains to man's nature ; and faith in part lifts up the veil which shrouds our Saviour and His Heavenly home ; giving glimpses of —1) His Blessed Person, " Whom not having seen " with the eye of the flesh ; but Whom having seen with the eye of faith ; " we love "—prophetic of that time when we " shall be like Him, and see Him as He is." 2) Of " the glory which shall be revealed in us ;" when we shall be clothed upon, and when mortality will be swallowed up of life. 3) Of the final condition of those who will " be turned into hell ;" having in this present life forgotten God. To bring vividly before a soul, all too bound to this fleeting time and life, the eternal realities of its everlasting condition, is the prophetic office of faith as a teacher.

II *Ennobling.*—To walk by sense is to live in one world instead of two. Faith reveals the ennobling vision of a spiritual world, by which we are surrounded. 1) Angels both good and evil. 2) Spirits and souls of the righteous ; " great cloud of witnesses " which are ever about our path. 3) The hidden charm and power of all the Sacraments, and other means of grace, which place us in a world of supernatural influences. Faith annimates a " letter that killeth," with " a spirit that giveth life."

III. *Real.*—The vision of faith is so real, that it has—1) Sustained Martyrs in their last moments. 2) Guided the Saints along the pathway of holiness. 3) Given a depth and earnestness to character, before unknown. It is no mere intellectual conception, but a living principle of life and action.

Epilogue.—The conditions of this spiritual life and teaching are, that we must first believe, and then we shall see. The heavenly vision is the reward of faith ; and in proportion to our faith will the brightness of this vision be—1) Clear ; 2) guiding ; 3) sustaining ; 4) joy-giving ; 5) transforming. (2 Cor. iii. 18.) Having this foretaste of the Beatific Vision, we can look over the intervening tract of sin, sorrow, and death ; and we can obtain a far-off sight of that Heavenly Canaan, in which can be recognized, in the land that is very far off, our Lord and Saviour, our God

and King, in His beauty, majesty, and glory ; whence
we gain also a glimpse of what our own future estate
will be, when we shall be like Him, when we shall see
Him as He is.

SERMON XLVIII.

HEAVEN THE LEGACY OF PEACE. *

"Peace I leave with you, My peace I give unto you."
—*S. John* xiv. 27.

S. Augustine.—" About to go away, 'peace I leave with you.' He will give to us His peace when He is about to come again at the end of the world. He leaves peace with us in this world; He will give us His peace in the world to come. He leaves peace with us, abiding in which we overcome the enemy; He will give us His peace when we shall reign without any enemy. He leaves peace with us, that even here we may mutually love; He will give us His peace when we never can dissent. He leaves His peace lest we should judge each other in our secret things, whilst we are in this world; He will give us His peace when He will make manifest the thoughts of the heart, and 'then shall every man have praise of God.' (1 Cor. iv. 5.) In Him, verily, and from Him is peace to us, whether He leaves it with us, about to go to

His Father; or whether He will give it to us when about to lead us to the Father. But what does He leave to us, when ascending from us, save Himself, whilst He departs not from us? 'For He is our peace Who hath made both one.' (Eph. ii. 14.) He, therefore, Himself is peace to us, both when we believe that He is; and when we see Him as He is."—*In Joan.* Tract lxxvii. vol. ix. p. 157, A.B.

This peace which our Blessed Lord left when He was going away was an earnest of that peace which He would not only leave behind Him, but also give in His kingdom and glory; and it draws the world of the future into close connection with the world of the present; so much so, that heaven itself may be said to be represented by this legacy of peace. This legacy and gift bring heaven home to us in its nearness by its present—

I. *Influence.*—Heaven is not so far off as we may sometimes deem it to be. It is true of the elect, "the Kingdom of God is within you." There is such a thing as a present heaven in which the first-fruits of that which is to be hereafter, can be tasted by us now. (*S. Aug. Confess.* lib. ix. c. 10. vol. i. p. 61, E.)

It is a great mistake to put the world unseen so far away from us as is so very often done. The holy live

under "the shadow of the Almighty." The influence
of the legacy of peace is noted in—1) The reconciliation
of God with man by the Cross. Man, who was some-
time afar from God, is now brought very nigh unto
Him. This reconciliation in its effects is but partial
now—the body of this death separates us from God—
it will be perfected when this legacy and gift of peace
is wholly ours, to be enjoyed without any stint or
hindrance. 2) In the true *mincha*, or peace offering,
which as His greatest legacy of peace the Lord left
behind Him in the Sacrament of the Altar. The
Holy Eucharist brings peace to the soul; since with
Its pardon It reveals to us the nearness of the kingdom
of heaven. Hence at the time of making our Communion, we are taught to sing:

> " Thou Thyself art dwelling
> In us at this hour."

3) In the guardianship of the holy Angels, who bring
a spiritual presence with them from heaven, and who
wait upon us, who are still abiding here on earth.
Many—in fact, all God's Saints—have both lived and
walked as if heaven were very nigh to them, for they
have seen it by the eye of faith.

II. *Associations.*—Have we never lost a relative, a
friend; one both near and dear to us? Who can say,
"I have not!" Smarting, then, under the sad

bereavement, the legacy of peace has softened the sorrow; such are not lost to us, but only gone before us; such, have but entered upon a new phase of the spiritual life; have been gathered into another fold of the great Church of God. These "spirits and souls of the righteous" bring the kingdom of heaven nigh to us indeed, for—1) our treasure is there; 2) our hope is there. We shall all be re-united some day.

III. *Actual Nearness.*—We cannot tell the minute, hour, day, or week of our translation into that kingdom of peace, in which we shall receive this legacy of peace in its perfection. They in whom "the peace of God which passeth all understanding" abides—the truly wise—ever hold themselves prepared to receive a sudden call, when the Master calls for them; and this perpetual and continuous preparation brings heaven down with a startling reality, close upon the confines f this daily life. Heaven becomes near to the soul in—1) Anticipation: it is entered in the spirit, before the actual presence is therein contained. 2) Effect: the peace of heaven is making a "great calm" upon the troubled billows of this world's stormy life. 3) Communion: near and dear with Him "Who is our peace."

Epilogue.—Live now in that faith and holiness, in that peace of Jesus which makes a present heaven of this earth; as being a true citizen of that heavenly country ; then at length shall the Lord's legacy of peace resolve itself into the New Jesusalem, that Vision of Peace which will be glorious, eternal, and perfect.

SERMON XLIX.

THE GUARDIANSHIP OF THE SOUL.

" Keep thy heart with all diligence, for out of it are the issues of life."—*Prov.* iv. 23.

S. Augustine.—" Sin is not simple ; it is not only wickedness, but it consists in admitting that which is forbidden."—*De Verâ Relig.* c. xxvi. vol. I. p. 276, A.

As well as a positive and an actual, there is a relative guilt in sin ; just as the most harmless meats or drinks may be very injurious, if not poisonous, when used in certain conditions of the body. Before the teaching of our Lord Jesus Christ, absolute sin was alone acknowledged, and then was only allowed to be sin when it had broken out in either word or deed. But He taught that the root of sin was within, that it lay in the heart ; that sin in thought was more to be guarded against, was more to be dreaded, than sin in word and action ; since the mind can be subject to no outward laws and has a certain liberty of its own, which makes it so very easy to sin in thought. Yes ! the admitting of that which is forbidden into the soul ; the allowing it there to germinate and leaven ; is indeed planting within the soul itself a root of bitterness. We must guard and pray against granting—

I. *A Presence of sin to the affections.*—The affections are prone to sin from several causes. 1) They fasten themselves upon visible objects ; they love the walk of sight rather than that of faith. Hence, they naturally place themselves upon the creature rather than upon the Creator; upon that which appeals to the senses, rather than to the higher principles of holiness and faith. They set up an idol in the heart, which is in itself a snare and a sin. 2) They strive to content themselves with the imperfect sympathies of this present life, during which they are but half revealed and half understood. They do not care to rise to the higher sympathy with the " Man of Sorrows." 3) They place the present before the future ; time before eternity ; earth before heaven. The presence of sin in the soul can be traced to one or other of these causes notwithstanding the infinite varieties of sin in thought, word, and deed.

II. *A Permission of sin by the will.*—Many sins, like sudden storms, overtake us all in times of sudden temptation, and weakness finds us all unprepared. Sudden temptation, sudden passion, sudden fear, bring a consequence with them that an after lifetime of repentance cannot wholly obliterate. By far the greater number, especially of our smaller sins, are permissive. The will consents to them. If the will were duly exercised they could not be committed, for it has the power to—1) Guard the avenues of the soul, which are the senses. 2) To discipline the affections. 3) To strengthen our every power of resistance.

III. *The Counsel of sin by the understanding.*— This is the most deadly form of sin, when the understanding takes counsel with itself to break God's revealed law; His moral law which is written in the conscience; and man's natural law which is founded upon justice. It renders man an outlaw to God; to himself; and to his fellow-man. All great crimes imply a planned wickedness; which proves—1) the dominion; 2) the habit; 3) the prostituting nature of sin.

Epilogue.—Oh! guard well, watchfully, and jealously the portals of the soul from the thought, word, look, and influence of sin. For when once it is admitted within the heart, it acts as a leaven, fermenting and corrupting the whole of the inner man; as a slow and subtle poison, altering and perverting all the natural functions and powers of the will, reason, memory, and affections; as a traitor within the camp, betraying all that is best and most sacred to the deadliest enemy and foe. Of what avail is it to guard the walls, when treason lurks within the citadel ? May the Lord's solemn warning ever be present to the memory in seasons of temptation, irresolution, and weakness : " Out of the heart proceed evil thoughts." (S. Matt. xv. 19.) "Out of the heart" that is not kept "with all diligence."

SERMON L.

WILL AND DEED.

" Whatsoever the Lord pleased, that did He."—*Ps.* cxxxv. 6.

S. Augustine.—" To will, and to be able to do, are two different things ; whence, neither he who wills is able immediately to do ; nor does he who is able to do, immediately will ; for as we sometimes will that which we are not able to perform, so also we are able sometimes to do that which we are unwilling to do. As therefore he who wills [vult] has the will [voluntas], so he who is able [potest] has the power, [potestatem.] But that anything may be done by the power, the will must be present."—*De Spirit. et Lit.* c. xxxi. vol. iii. p. 280, A.

The whole ground of life and action is covered by these few and simple words. They embrace alike the perfection of God and the estate of lost and ruined creatures ; they probe to the very depths of thought and action ; they bring before us most plainly and forcibly the three estates, to one of which we must belong; they represent to man his own starting-point, and his lawful progress. In them we note those who—

I. *Will and can.*—This is the highest and perfect state; it belongs to God alone, in Whom the will and power to do, are united. "Whatsoever the Lord pleased," or willed, "that did He." So in our Blessed Lord's miracles. "I will, be thou whole." "God which worketh in you both to will and to do of His good pleasure." (Phil. ii. 13.) This marvellous combination of will and power brings some of the other attributes of God out into a bold relief. Consider—1) God's creative, conservative, and redemptive providences; the adaptation of means to end; the schemes of man, the universe, of the worlds outside, and far beyond our solar system. God made all things, and ordered all things as He willed: the result is law, harmony, and beauty. Had an imperfect creature this union of will and power, how horrible and terrible would be the result; but God wills in perfect wisdom, as He does or acts in infinite power. Hence our gain in submitting ourselves to His all-powerful and wise will. 2) That with God, thought is action; the desire or will includes its accomplishment; so that God must be necessarily complete in Himself; as He imagines and conceives, so He is.

" Who then by searching can find out God ?" save he whose mind is as great as is the mind of God. We learn to bow in holy reverence before the Divine Majesty of His Person.

II. *Will and cannot.*—This represents our present state of human imperfection, in which " to will is present with me; but how to perform that which is good I find not. (Rom. vii. 18.) This sad schism between thought and action accounts in great part for that which we see in the world of—1) Inconsistency. Desire and will run beyond the power of their fulfilment. Men aim high, but fall low; they desire holiness, yet are ever falling into sin. Life is, therefore, one continuous struggle and combat ; a perpetual seeking to realize an ideal state, which weakness, sin, and sorrow, render an impossibility here on earth. 2) Unhappiness. When the will has far outstripped the power, disappointment, nay, despair, cannot but follow. Desiring great things, small things alone become ours ; things, which convey in their very presence a keen sense of defeat and weakness. 3) Unproductiveness of life. I cannot attain my desires, why then should I struggle and strive in vain ? My goal is beyond me ; I will not compete for a lesser prize. Earnest souls who will and cannot, are ever receiving help from above ; so that the Christian ideal, in part realized here, may be altogether realized hereafter. The agonizing seeker after holiness, love, and knowledge, receives the Saviour's promise : " My grace is sufficient for thee" (2 Cor. xii. 9), and thereby is comforted.

III. *Can and will not.*—This condition pertains to—1) Devils and lost spirits ; endowed with power, yet wasting will. 2) To those who squander and idle away the precious season of this present life. Such a state implies—1) the severest punishments ; 2) the highest form of self-reproach ; 3) an unthankful neglect of means and opportunity.

Epilogue.—Pass onwards and upwards, O Christian soul, from power to desire ; and from desire again to power and will united ; from sin to the desire, and struggle after such holiness as thou mayest be able to attain. Know then it is thy glorious prerogative to be able to do all things through Christ Who strengtheneth thee ; that whilst there is one sin to be conquered ; one desire to be subdued ; one step toward Heaven to be gained ; there is one more jewel to be earned by thee ; there is one more glory to be added to thy Heavenly crown.

London: SWIFT & Co., 1 to 5, Newton Street, High Holborn, W.C.